MW01065498

Evil
Entombed

Edwina Groat

Copyright © 2018 by Edwina Groat

All rights reserved. No part of this book may
be reproduced or transmitted in any form or by
any means, electronic or mechanical, including
photocopying, recording, or any information
storage and retrieval system, without permission in
writing from the author.

ISBN: 978-1-948638-94-4

PUBLISHED BY

Fideli Publishing, Inc.
119 W. Morgan St.
Martinsville, IN 46151

www.FideliPublishing.com

PRINTED IN THE UNITED STATES OF AMERICA

Prologue

It had been a year of triumph and tragedy for Zoe. There'd been the untimely death of her father, was driven to complete his plans to revive a once great city left to rot and decay. Then, the near collapse of her father's engineering firm, fomented by Nelson R. Beckman, a corrupt and immoral financier capable of unspeakable acts of violence, bribery and deceit. That was just the beginning of Zoe's descent into torment.

The biggest nightmare had been the discovery of multiple sets of human remains at her father's jobsite. Investigation into this had unveiled a decades' old secret, unsolved murders, and the near death and paralysis of her husband Garth. All of this had brought her to the edge of insanity.

Salvation came in the form of Nelson Beckman's attorney, Josh Lawton, who became Zoe's unlikely ally. He was the one who finally broke Beckman's stronghold. Once that happened and Beckman died, all manner of evil stopped surrounding Zoe. As Beckman's trustee, Josh had made things right.

Zoe gave thanks and reviewed her blessings daily. Garth was healthy, the project was successful, the company was prosperous, and the grieving parents of the murdered children were given closure.

Evil had been put on hold, for now...

Chapter 1

Zoe fell back in the large easy chair in front of the fire as the October sunlight splintered through the leaded glass windows. She hugged her coffee mug close, and it brought comforting warmth to her hands and face. It was hard to believe it had been almost a year since she'd first explored this old place, and now it was everything she had hoped for in a home.

The past year had been filled with new beginnings and welcome endings for those in her life, as well as death, darkness, hate, redemption, new love and healing. The thought of almost losing the business to a maniacal corrupt murderer, a freak accident almost taking Garth from her on top of the loss of her father ... it made her head spin when she thought about it.

But the addition of new and dear friends, comforting neighbors, the salvaged lives of three children saved from life on the streets, and an end to all the misery, greed and misunderstanding that had seemed to coalesce in a Shakespearean tale made it all worthwhile. The devil got his due, and all the pain and suffering he caused came to an end. Nelson R. Beckman was dead, and everything that followed had been good.

Zoe stretched broadly and yawned. Garth was sleeping in this Sunday morning, and she was enjoying the solitude and gentle crackle of the fire. Recovering from Rachel's pig-fest and neighborhood gathering yesterday called for a full day of lounging.

The arrival of three children to Rachel's home last year had turned the senior citizen into a youthful dynamo. It was like Josh's mother had discovered the fountain of youth. She was on the move all the time — planning, singing, cooking, playing, riding, and come spring, Zoe had promised her they'd learn to play golf.

Rachel had also become a good neighbor and friend, and in many ways she was the mother Zoe longed for after losing her mother at an early age.

Josh, Rachel's son, had become so enamored with Zoe's cousin Maggie — and her dog — that she felt honored she'd played matchmaker. Josh was perfectly smitten, and their many visits to Rachel's frequently meant dinner at the Lawton house with she and Maggie taking cooking direction from Rachel, while Garth and Josh watched a game, bet, told lies and talked about new projects. Business was good — life was good. God is in His heaven and all is right with the world.

"Woman of the house!" Zoe was pulled from her thoughts by Garth's playful roar from the top of the stairs. "I smell coffee."

"Well come on down, master of the house. I'll pour you a cup. I might even make you a hearty breakfast if you're nice, and you're willing to listen to some ideas I have about the house."

"Oh, noooo! I'll be nice, and patient, if I must. But please, please give me five minutes after that hearty breakfast before we start talking about our house from hell."

"Oh, stop it," she scolded. As much as Garth complained about their old house, she knew he was "into it." His "I can do anything" contractor patience was wearing thin, though. Zoe had to admit she could be a bit like a dog with a bone about the house. "Okay, no talk about the house 'til after breakfast in our beautiful new kitchen."

At that moment, they heard the huge lion door-knocker banging on their newly refurbished 10-foot oak front door. Zoe answered it, and there stood Josh, putter in hand and a large grin on his face. "Anyone for golf? It's a little chilly, but I'm taking the boys over to chip a few."

"Saved by the bell," Garth said, chuckling.

"Oh, you two had this planned," she grumbled.

"Say, Josh, as my personal attorney, business manager and confidant, is it possible to get an annulment after a year of marriage? It seems my wife and this house have become one."

"Oh, you. Go get your clothes on, and I'll get you some coffee. Josh, you want some?"

"No, thanks. I've had my quota," he said as he followed her into the kitchen.

Looking around, Josh whistled approvingly, as he smoothed his hand over the finely crafted cabinets and counters. "Sure has come a long way from the first time I saw this white elephant."

"Yes, it has, and I love every square foot of the place." Before she could go into a laundry list of renovation ideas with Josh, Garth came to the rescue, wearing his lucky shirt. He was ready for revenge,since Josh had won the last go 'round at the course.

"You're not winning today," Garth said, as they hurried out the door. Zoe could hear Josh crowing about his last victory as they went to the car, and hoped Garth shot a 100 as payment for his Sunday deception.

She blew him a kiss, closed the mighty door, and retreated to the kitchen to pour herself another cup of coffee. As she walked by teh French doors, she let Hugo, the family's Great Dane, back inside.

Afterward, she made her way to the study. Burrowing deep into her comfy chair with Hugo at her feet, she re-launched her quest for the perfect bed and bath, sifting through piles and piles of *House Beautiful* and *Architectural Digest*.

They'd decided to remodel the house while living in it. Some thought it best to stay in town while all the work was done, but Zoe insisted on "living the dream." Unfortunately, as Garth had predicted so many months ago, it did at times turn into a nightmare of inconvenience and short tempers were the result.

The kitchen was finally finished, and it was worth it because it was now the jewel of the home.

Its beauty was currently jealously guarded by thick sheets of plastic that cut it off from all the construction dust and mayhem.

The majority of the home was still covered in contracting tools, tarps and debris. Outside, the scaffolding had been up for several weeks, because the tuck-pointing was being held hostage by the whims of weather. The contractor's unending excuses and dealing with his other jobs were also slowing things down. Breathing dust, toxic fumes, and the constant whining of power tools had became the norm, and she hardly noticed anymore.

Zoe would not admit to Garth how unnerving it was to be there all day with everything going on around her. That would be too much like admitting she'd made a mistake. She just knew this would be the "Mona Lisa" of homes when it was finished, so she'd stick it out to the end. When she felt overwhelmed by the men constantly under foot, she retreated to a small alcove upstairs where she'd stashed her computer, TV, and some good books.

Friday it had started to rain again about noon, and of course, all work ceased. The plumber, plasterer, roofer and the rest of the crew all sang the same refrain about more delays. All she could say was, "Yes. Yes. I understand. I'll see you all on Monday."

She'd decided that no more construction for the day meant it was a perfect time to cook an experimental dinner. Just like everything else that day, it was a failure and they'd ordered Chinese.

Coming out of her thoughts, she said, "Well, it looks like it's just you and me, Hugo." She stroked his massive head, and added, "You think I should make something nice for dinner?"

She got up and headed into her new kitchen, closing the heavy plastic divider behind her. Soon, she had the makings of a hearty stew going. It was Garth's favorite. *I'll have dinner waiting, hot and steamy, when he gets back*, she thought. *Stew's just the ticket for a cold winter evening.*

When she finished putting the stew together, she found she was at a loss for something to do. She hated how long the days seemed since she'd removed herself from the everyday mechanics of the office. She missed being a part of the inner workings. Garth kept her up to date, but it wasn't the same.

When the two wayward men came through the door later that afternoon, they were discussing

Josh's plans to enlarge and enhance the radio station he'd turned over to Beckman's widow, Julie. "She's taken to it like a duck to water," Josh said, as the rosy-cheeked pair came through the door.

When Garth saw Zoe, he said, "My lucky shirt worked! Josh had to pay me a dollar and I got to shame him for shooting a 90."

"Yeah, I'll be victorious next time. I want a rematch, but right now I need to get going."

"Your humiliation practically drove him out of the house," Zoe commented as she shut the door after Josh made his exit.

Garth grinned. "That quick exit was because of your cousin, Maggie, not me. He's meeting her tonight. You certainly started a fire there. He's crazy about her."

"Oh, that's wonderful! Wedding bells soon?"

"Wouldn't be surprised."

"Oh? Tell me what else he said."

"Oh, no. You'll have to find out for yourself next time you see her. A gentleman never gossips."

"What do you mean? Men are bigger gossips than women ever could be. Now come on, give."

"Okay, okay." Garth briefed her on the "Romance of Maggie and Garth," telling her just enough to make her stop pestering him.

Garth's mood was happy, and Zoe was not about to spoil it with more talk about the house.

As they headed to the kitchen, the alluring aroma sent him into a culinary rapture. Poking his nose over the pot he remarked, "Rachel certainly has made you a better cook."

"Chuck, that's the secret in stew."

"Come here, my little stew-maker," he teased. "You *cook* in many, many ways."

She grinned broadly, and he took his seat at the head of the table, ready for a heaping bowl.

They spent the rest of the afternoon and evening lazily, indulging in good food and good wine.

Chapter 2

Unfortunately, Monday morning's weather was a repeat of Friday, with rain pelting the windows of the old house in the pre-dawn hours. Zoe and Garth knew immediately it would be all no-shows on the construction front today. The calls, from the "butcher, the baker and candlestick maker" came in early, with everyone voicing their regrets about not working for the day.

"Looks like you've got another day to yourself. It's just you and Hugo, again."

"We're both going back to sleep." *It's just as well. I'm not in the mood for screaming power tools, drywall dust, plasterers and plumbers today.*

At two o'clock, Zoe drove the few miles over to Rachel's for a visit. She was Josh's mother and Zoe viewed her as her adopted mom and good friend. Rachel would sit patiently listening to Zoe's constant ramblings about the renovation for hours on end. On occasion, she'd throw in an idea worth considering. Zoe loved that she had someone to talk to who was actually interested, since Garth was getting tired of hearing about it.

Zoe waltzed into Rachel's kitchen and bellied up to the big island bar in her kitchen. Her friend was ready for her. "Here, try some — your favorite, chicken salad with grapes and walnuts."

"You're a mind reader, Rach. I'm starving."

"Well what's next on the agenda?" Rachel couldn't wait for the next blow-by-blow description of the next steps in the renovation of the White Elephant of Suffolk County, i.e. Zoe's house.

Understanding that she had a willing listener, Zoe paused, sandwich in hand, and started rhapsodizing about her grand oak staircase, listing every curve and carving etched in its long, elegant flight to the second floor. Next, they talked about the refurbished chandeliers, windows and doors leading to the new landscaped fairy tale waterfall and woods. The way she went on, you'd think Zoe was talking about Versailles.

Rachel was glad things were going well for Zoe. It was a pleasure to see her so happy and full of purpose.

When Rachel started to fill her wine glass for a third time, Zoe waved the bottle away, stood up and hugged Rachel. "Thank you for listening to me, you're a good friend. I know I've been a terrible bore."

"No, dear, I love your enthusiasm and your company. I'm just happy you didn't accept that third glass of wine." They both threw their heads back and laughed.

Chapter 3

Tuesday morning broke depressing and gray, with the first snow of the season falling, intermixed with rain and sleet. The accompanying wind, driven down from the north, cut through the white flakes so they didn't settle. Obviously, the scaffolding would embrace the house in its skeletal wrap for yet another day, leaving the brick and mortar untouched by workmen until weather was more agreeable. The inevitable no-show calls came in early.

Even the architect had re-scheduled their meeting for the following day at one o'clock. Zoe wanted some ideas about putting a balcony outside the second floor master bedroom, so it would overlook the beautiful grounds. She thought that idea sounded perfect. She also wanted to discuss what to do with the basement now that the old monster water heater and furnace had been removed.

She went downstairs to check on the muriatic acid scrubbing she'd ordered for the white bedrock. It had uncovered some lovely stone graphics. The north wall where she envisioned putting the wine cooler, however, had stubbornly refused to give up its mold and mildew. *I can't believe that slimy ooze has come back, even after the second acid bath. Oh well, that wall will probably have to be replaced when they install the cooler. I guess it won't matter.*

She turned to shut off the light just as something caught Hugo's attention. The dog's head was cocked and his ears were on-point. He was wearing a quizzical look on his face, and Zoe's look mirrored his. Straining hard to hear, she realized there was a faint sound like a piccolo at the beginning of a polonaise, building to a crescendo. Human and canine both shook their heads, puzzled.

The warmth of the fireplace upstairs soon lured both from the damp cloister of the cellar, and the mystery sound was forgotten.

Chapter 4

Wednesday dawned bright and clear, and everyone showed up for work. Soon, the house began to buzz with carpenters, plasterers and painters. Even the scaffolding outside showed signs of life, with tuck-pointers dotting the skeletal ladder like notes on a musical staff. The grand old dame was again immersed in her rehabilitation.

Zoe was anxiously waiting for the jackhammers to clear out and enlarge the area for the wine cooler in the cellar. The cooler itself was going to be delivered next week, and she wanted everything to be complete before it arrived. Unfortunately, the electrician had yet to complete the hook-ups, so the schedule was looking iffy.

Tim, the foreman, called her down to show her something he'd uncovered. He'd thought he was breaking through a solid wall of rock, but what he found was far less difficult to remove. About two feet in, there was an open area, about four feet square, where ancient timbers covered what seemed to be an old well.

The wood was rotted and made the covering far too fragile to kneel on and accurately get measurements of the well's depth. Zoe heeded Tim's warning about the safety of the area as she walked to where he was pointing. She just shook her head, disappointed by yet another aggravating setback.

The crew had pulled all the rock and debris from the area, and Tim was quick to announce that he felt his job was done. "Call me after talking to your architect," he said over his shoulder as he walked away. "I'll be busy for the next three to six weeks, so call soon to get on my schedule.

Zoe noticed that Tim and his crew seemed to be in a hurry to go, but didn't think much of it. She followed them outside and told them she'd be in touch.

When she went back inside, she headed downstairs again. She was distracted as she surveyed the area, thinking about her plans and how to handle this latest hurdle. *It certainly looks like there's more than enough open space for what I want to do. That well isn't going to slow us down. The architect can surely figure out a way to deal with it.*

As she moved closer to the recently opened maw of the stone wall, she felt the temperature drop. A clammy cold enveloped her, and she suddenly felt like she had a fever, and suddenly felt the need to vomit as a paralyzing feeling of foreboding enveloped her. It was the same feeling she'd once felt when she was asked go to the city morgue to identify a young woman she'd known in college. The memory of that feeling had never left her, and nothing could compare to it.

She quickly left the cellar for the fresh air above, and went to the kitchen to poured a glass of wine to settle her nerves. *Maybe I've caught a winter flu bug,* she thought as she shivered.

The rest of the contractors were still hard at work, and they were everywhere. Zoe headed to her secluded retreat to stay out of their way. The heavy sweater she'd pulled on earlier failed to stop the cold chills reverberating through her body.

I have to be getting sick, she thought as she grabbed her phone to call Garth and ask him to stop and get the "green stuff" on his way home. As she ended the call, she was hit with a headache and then felt nauseous again. *Thank goodness the crews and their racket will be gone soon.*

By the time Garth got home, the workers had been gone for over an hour. Zoe had found her way to the large easy chair in front of the fire and Hugo was laying at her feet. Garth greeted a pale Zoe with a quick kiss and a hand to her forehead to check for fever.

After that, he unloaded what seemed to be a mini-pharmacy: green stuff, red stuff, blue stuff, decongestants of all kinds, aspirin, Alka-Seltzer, Advil and several boxes of tissues. It seemed he'd called out the pharmaceutical equivalent of a military "scorched earth, take no prisoners" policy for the intruding germs. He'd also picked up Chinese for dinner.

Zoe declined the food in favor of plenty of ice water, which was her main course throughout the evening. She felt a bit better just watching Garth enjoy his General Tso chicken.

After taking the "green stuff," she fell soundly asleep. Garth didn't want to disturb her and spent the rest of the night on the oversized sofa.

He awoke early, as usual, the next morning, and immediately checked on his still-sleeping wife. She appeared to have spent a fitful night, and looked pale and feverish.

The workmen were going to show up any minute, so Garth called Josh and then Rachel. Gently he roused Zoe, gathered her flu artillery, and drove her to Rachel's house, where a bleary-eyed Zoe was immediately guided to the quiet solitude of the guest room.

"Back, under the covers for you," Garth said. "Get some rest. I'm going back to the house to get a solid date for completion. Looks like there are only loose ends left to be finished up, and I want to hurry it along."

Garth was right. There wasn't that much more to do to wrap up, so Zoe weakly agreed and took another shot of the "green stuff," apologized to Rachel for being such a bother, and promptly went back to sleep.

Garth hugged Rachel and thanked her for watching Zoe, as he was headed out the door.

"I'll take good care of her. Now, you go on about your business."

Knowing Zoe was in good hands and would be able to get some rest, Garth returned to the house to coordinate the final finishing touches. On the way home, he called and asked Mrs. Potter, his most loyal "gal Friday" and assistant, if she could hold the fort for the next couple of days.

Mrs. Potter had been with Zoe's father, Warren, from the beginning and knew the business inside out. If Warren was the heart of the business, Mrs. Potter was its soul. After he took over, Garth wondered sometimes who worked for who.

"Don't worry about a thing," she told him. "Take care of Zoe, and get that house done."

Garth could've been in the Swiss Alps and he wouldn't worry because he knew the business was in good hands. He told Mrs. Potter if she or Norm, his foreman, needed anything, he'd have his cell.

When he returned home, he saw the painters and roofers were already scaling the grand old dame's turrets. He found the general contractor and pulled him aside for a heart to heart regarding the current condition of each facet of the project and demanded an estimated time of completion.

Joe, the contractor who had worked for Garth for years, seemed unwilling to commit to a date. He listed the weather, the workers, the shipments, and multiple other excuses as his excuse.

"All of the special orders except the wine cooler are here," Garth parried. "The first and second floor need to be completed and ready for occupancy by next Tuesday. That's one week from today."

Joe had worked for Garth enough over the years to know when he'd been given an ultimatum, so he went off to motivate his crew. Suddenly the clatter, rattle and clunk of workmen's tools reached a new crescendo. It seemed the tune around the old house had changed from "Taps" to "Reveille."

Garth liked the change in tempo.

Chapter 5

The following Tuesday morning was bright, clear, and beautiful, with the temperature hovering at just above freezing. Garth picked up Zoe promptly at 10 a.m. and drove her the few miles their Long Island home. She could barely keep her eyes open against the bright sun, but finally got a glimpse of the house as she squinted.

The "Boy on a Dolphin" fountain in the middle of the circular driveway was the first thing she noticed. Squealing, she thought, *This is the most beautiful home in the whole wide world!*

Gone were the wheelbarrows, stacks of bricks, plaster encrusted plastic tarps, miscellaneous equipment and concrete mixers. Replacing them was a beautifully landscaped entrance with freshly laid sod, mulched evergreens and large Tuscan pots filled with small evergreens framing the beautiful oak front door. The large brass lion's head doorknocker was brightly polished, and his great mane sparkled in the sunshine.

As she was squealing in un-intelligible gibberish, Garth picked Zoe up and whisked her over the threshold — something he hadn't done on their wedding day a year ago. While holding her, he spun in a wide circle so she could appreciate everything.

The foyer floor had been replaced with a classic black and white granite tile. It was beautiful. Garth put her down so she could explore. Everything was just as she'd dreamed it would be. Erica, the designer, had brought all the colors and furnishings together into one cohesive "ahh!"

Suddenly, Josh and Maggie popped out of the kitchen with a bottle of champagne. "Welcome home, Zoe!" they chorused. Maggie hugged Zoe warmly, while Garth and Josh retreated to parts unknown, with Hugo on their heels. The ladies were left to ooh and ahh over the large kitchen counter, and the quarry tile steps outside the French doors. The quality of workmanship on the exterior was superior.

After 45 minutes of inspections and investigative talk, Josh and Garth returned to find the girls already planning a housewarming. This was a new chapter in their lives and Zoe wanted to document it with a party. Maggie and Josh left shortly after, leaving the two to "get to know" their new house.

"Oh, isn't it grand? Beautiful, grandly beautiful or beautifully grand?" she twittered like a child over a new pony. She couldn't believe Garth had got the workmen to finish it up without her.

She hugged Garth and thanked him for dealing with all the aggravating loose ends. "Everything is perfect! I wouldn't change a thing. That nasty old flu turned into a blessing for me. I feel wonderful."

"I hope this means I won't have to hear one more idea about this house. It's time to turn this place into a home."

"I promise, " she said. "You won't hear another peep about it from me. Consider the rehab conversations put to bed."

A little while later, Garth retreated to his new study to do a little paperwork and prep for the next day. This last week dealing with the house had put him a little behind.

Zoe, left to her own devices, opened her new patio doors and stepped out into her fairy tale backyard. The small cold-water creek with its soft streaming waterfalls danced pleasantly down from the hillside. The sound was magical.

The enveloping shadows of the evening made it colder, so Zoe turned to go inside. As she turned, she noticed the silhouette of a large animal at the top of the hill. When she moved to look closer, it vanished. *That looked like a wolf — a very large wolf. That can't be*, she thought. *Evening shadows and the fog can be very confusing and tricky. That has to be all it was.*

Zoe turned again to go inside and felt a wave of "it's good to be home" feelings. She went inside and snuggled up in her big easy chair to watch an old Turner Classic movie.

Chapter 6

The great wolf lay in the shadows, his massive head held alert and watchful, as his penetrating blue eyes surveyed his surroundings. He was a monstrous wolf, with a coat of misty gray-white that blended into the dusky evening shadows. He was alone, as wolves are sometimes known to live, and the lesser animals of the woods didn't seem to fear him. It had been over two centuries since he'd last been summoned.

The patience in his demeanor suggested the steadfast stance of a sentry, alert to all possibilities. The beast's name was of no consequence; it had been known by many. Just as good and evil had existed since time began, so, too, had the wolf.

Evil is near. The watchful eyes of the huge creature were staring directly at Zoe's new home. *Evil never dies, it rests, it takes a holiday, it can be held in remission or contained, but it cannot die,* the wolf thought. *It comes in many forms, and I know that soon this particular evil will be released.*

It was true. The renovation and resulting disturbance surrounding Garth and Zoe's home had uncovered something evil. For more than 250 years the soul of a murderous fellow named Cedric Bradford had been held in limbo. Now it was free.

In life, Bradford was so completely devoid of morals and respect for human life that to be rid of him, England had sent him to the colonies to suppress uprisings by the Indians and colonists. Many were assigned by King George to suppress unrest, but he was by far the most vile.

The particularly heinous and medieval forms of torture known drawing and quartering and flogging delighted Bradford. He treated any of the misfortunates who stood against the Crown in the smallest of ways to these tortures. Being shot forthwith was a kindness he rarely dealt out.

The crown had given him carte blanche to deal with the problem "by whatever means necessary," and he took full advantage. During the war, men on both sides came to fear his name. Non-military husbands, wives and children, as well as Native Americans who stood in the way of his efforts to "quell any uprising" were shown no mercy. Neither soldiers nor civilians were exempt from his hellish wrath.

He was lean, tall and imperious — it showed in his dress and demeanor. His cold black stare blazed out from atop his slim, patrician nose. He was cruel to animals and soldiers alike, and his wrath rained down at the smallest infraction.

He was cunning and enlisted help from married men from the colonies, encouraging them to report anything suspicious or face the consequences. Besides his love of torture, he also liked to burn things — homes, churches, barns. He stole from residents and destroyed farmer's fields. He committed murder in the name of God and country, but his rampages were solely to feed his bloodlust and need for power and control.

Many soldiers under his command feared for their lives should his orders not be carried out to the letter. His behavior furthered the hate, fear and loathing for the British throughout the colonies.

There was with a collective sigh of relief from both sides when the maniacal and heartless life of Cecil Bradford came to an end one fine October day in 1775. He was killed by a gray wolf in the shadow of an ancient oak as he dismounted from his horse outside the village square.

Bradford's sword found its mark, wounding the wolf on its haunch. That barely slowed the wolf's attach, and no soldier or civilian tried to save him from this unusual "natural disaster." The great beast was doing them a favor, so they allowed the animal safe passage to the woods.

Bradford's bloodied body was unceremoniously stripped and thrown into the village well located near a patriot's home that he'd recently burned down. News of Bradford's death spread, and the well and surrounding area became a bit of a sideshow.

The British searched for their missing officer, and the locals knew the unsolved death would certainly invite unwanted questions. The stench from the open well had to be dealt with before anyone figured out its source. The citizens brought straw, whale oil, candles, saplings and aged wood to the well, threw it in and set it on fire. When it had burned itself out, they filled the hole with rock and sealed it.

No one said a prayer over the deceased. The wolf watched it all as he nursed his wound in the shadows.

Chapter 7

Garth left early that morning; he was still adjusting to his morning commute. Zoe slept in a bit, but got up in time to give Garth a goodbye hug. She told him she'd meet him in the afternoon after she'd picked up some things at Macys.

They were going to meet Maggie and Josh for dinner. They couple had said they had something to discuss. Zoe hoped it would be a wedding announcement.

With Hugo at her side, Zoe grabbed her boots, coat and coffee. She opened the French doors and Hugo lunged out, headed to the woods to perform his daily routine. Zoe, as had become her habit, completed a walk around the property's edge while she waited for him. The day shone bright and crisp, with all remaining leaves reflecting gold, red and various burnt orange hues.

As the cold air filled her lungs, waking up her senses, she thought, *I feel alive out here.* She followed the fall of the water along the edge of the spring, then called out for Hugo, who was checking out a rabbit's den. When he heard her call, he started running with a fluid, graceful gait.

Suddenly, cold fear came over man and beast in tandem. In the open field, a massive New England Copperhead reared its serpentine head, maw wide-open and fangs showing. The snake made a purposeful advance toward Zoe, showing no fear. The serpent raised its head and seemed to glare at her. Icy fear gripped her soul, and she was unable to move or speak.

Hugo, recovering from his paralysis, went into protective mode and charged toward the vile intruder attacking his master. Then, like a shadow appearing at twilight, the wolf was suddenly between Hugo and Zoe, deftly destroying the serpent by removing its head.

Hugo didn't seem to find this new intruder dangerous or offending, and the wolf lay the remains of the snake at his feet in an unspoken alliance. The wolf turned away from Hugo, casually approached Zoe, and sat down in front of her. Its blue eyes stared into hers, almost reassuringly. After making its unspoken introduction, the wolf disappeared into the shadows in the woods.

Shaking uncontrollably, Zoe sank to her knees, gulping in cool, sobering gasps of fresh air. Hugo stood by, giving comfort as best he could. Zoe hugged the dog and used his great breadth to help herself stand. Briefly looking at the carcass of the copperhead, woman and dog ran directly through the patio doors and into the house. Zoe turned around and locked the doors securely behind them.

Breathing deeply, Zoe collapsed into her easy chair by the fire and shuddered, trying to regain her "sea legs." The fire warmed her, and eventually she got up to make some coffee. When the coffee was done and poured, she began to feel normal again.

After she finished her coffee, she called Garth and told him she would see him round 6:30, but didn't tell him about the snake.

Happy hour talk tonight with Maggie and Josh certainly won't be dull, she thought later, as she was getting dressed.

Outside, two large reptiles entwined themselves beneath the statue in the fountain. As Zoe drove away, the late afternoon shone brilliantly on the copper colored leaves, as two more snakes made their way to the fountain.

Chapter 8

Zoe, who'd been busy buying small necessities for her new home all day, had almost put the morning's events behind her by the time Garth called to say he'd meet Josh, Maggie and her for a few beers and burgers at Sal's after he returned a few calls. She'd lost track of time and couldn't believe it was almost six.

Zoe hoped to hear good news about her cousin Maggie, and Josh. Soon after Maggie moved to New York, Zoe had invited her to visit and then introduced her to Josh at a barbecue he'd hosted at his mother Rachel's house.

Life certainly had a funny way of turning things around. She hadn't liked Josh at all in the beginning. Francis Harralday, her father's corporate attorney for the past 30 years, decided to retire to Florida to live the good life with his wife and a basset hound named Zeke. After careful consideration, he'd turned Erskine and Avery's corporate affairs over to the firm of Lawton and Lawton with his blessing, and Josh Lawton had been proud to accept.

Josh was Beckman's attorney, too, at the time, which made him a villain in Zoe's eyes. As she got to know him, though, she found out he wasn't a bad guy. He ultimately had a great deal to do with the completion of Zoe's father's project, and that put him firmly in the good guy category. Seeing her father's prized and noble rebuilding plans for decaying neighborhoods become a reality was really satisfying. Garth, his young partner, well chosen by Warren had kept his promise to see the dream fulfilled.

Her father would've been proud to see new schools, the community center and the manufacturing facilities spring to life; all in spite of Beckman. She would forever be grateful to Josh for this, and was sorry she'd initially judged him by the man he represented rather than on his on merit.

It was pretty funny that she'd been briefly romantically attracted to Josh. Looking back on it now, she knew that feeling was simply her heart telling her she could trust him.

It was hard to believe someone who worked for the man Zoe, Garth and her father hated most could end up being a such good friend. Now, she loved him like a brother and best friend, and eagerly looked forward to him becoming a part of her faimly.

She just knew he and Maggie were going to announce their engagement at Sal's that evening. *Josh and Maggie deserve all the happiness in the world,* she thought. Plans for the wedding were already dancing in her head. *They can have it here at the house, in my fairy tale garden.*

Zoe remembered fondly the day she'd dragged Josh along on yet another one of her house-hunting trips. He just happened to be at the office and got drafted to be Garth's stand-in for the day after he was called away to deal with business. Josh had gone with Zoe to look at the Long Island house that had become her new home. "See that she doesn't do anything crazy,"

Garth had pleaded as they left. As it turned out, this was the day she'd found her dream house and another new friend —Josh's mother, Rachel.

There was a line of people waiting for seats when she got to Sal's, but Zoe saw Maggie's hand pop up, guiding her to seats by the window. "Wow, this place seems busy for a Tuesday night," she commented to Maggie, as she gave her a hug. "Have you ordered yet? I'm starved."

Zoe squeezed in next to Garth, hugging him, too. They chatted happily, each giving a blow-by-blow accounting of their days, with Zoe contributing an animated retelling of the snake incident.

Finally, Zoe looked suspiciously at Maggie, and said, "I thought there was something you two wanted to talk about."

Maggie looked coyly at Zoe, teasing her, then finally revealed her left hand, which sported a giant "rock." She waved her hand back and forth so the stone caught the light.

"I knew it!" Zoe squealed. She looked at both men, who were just grinning and taking it all in. "You both knew, didn't you?"

"Congratulations, Maggie. He's definitely a keeper," Garth said.

A bottle of Champagne soon made its way to their table along with their burgers.

What the hell, burgers and champagne it is, Zoe thought.

Chapter 9

nother nasty morning, Jesus! It seems like the weather is never gonna clear up, Zoe thought. She had awakened with a mission — shoring up the hole down in the cellar so the wine cooler could be installed. *I've put off the delivery of the cooler twice now. That's enough!*

The rest of the house was finished, and she loved it. *I wish I'd never started the whole wine cooler business.* Her irritation with the cooler was compounded by an awful headache and a bad case of dry mouth.

Garth must've known she'd feel this way, because there was a large pitcher of ice water and a glass of orange juice waiting for her on the table beside the bed. "Oh, thank you, thank you, thank you! The honeymoon is *not* over!"

"Yeah, well don't get used to it," he said as he kissed her playfully. "I'm off. ... Love you!" Garth motioned to Hugo. "Come on, boy. I'll let you out."

"Give me a call if you need anything. Hopefully, Baylor can figure out what to do with the mess in the cellar."

"Oh, God, I forgot all about him!"

"The architect said he'd be here sometime before noon, too. He did say he'd call before he comes.

Zoe swooned back into her pillow. "Okay, I'll get up."

Zoe reluctantly followed Garth downstairs and out the door to wave him off. She let Hugo out and decided she was not in the mood for an early morning walk after the peculiar snake incident the day before. Besides, she had to deal with the cellar and wine cooler business. Somehow, the idea just didn't appeal as much now. *I just want the whole mess done and gone.*

Zoe went to the cellar and saw there was a tarp covering the hole. Little orange cones and yellow caution tape surrounded it. The whole atmosphere of the area had changed from the cozy hideaway she'd first encountered to something more sinister.

Baylor arrived around 10:30, and Zoe greeted him with an offer of iced tea or coffee. She also imparted the urgency she felt about getting the project finished as soon as possible. None of the workmen had been down to the cellar since they'd discovered the well behind the wall.

They headed down to inspect the area. "Anyone have any idea how deep this thing goes?" Baylor asked, as he peered cautiously into the hole.

"Not that I know of. The crew left, and won't be back until we figure out what to do. I just want this done and over with."

"Well, we could fill it with gravel or concrete, or simply cover it with a steel plate capable of supporting the weight of the cooler."

Zoe told him to go with whatever was most expeditious and cost-effective. At this point, she had an overwhelming urge to just get the heck out of the cellar. Baylor seemed to be feeling it, too.

He'd always thought this space was creepy, however he hadn't mentioned it to Zoe. Before they left, he couldn't resist picking up a rock and tossing it down the hole. They waited to hear the rock hit bottom or at least splash into water, but they heard nothing.

Baylor quickly covered the hole with the tarp and set the caution cones back in place. By the time he was finished, Zoe was already halfway up the steps. As she climbed, she noticed that the black mold-like substance on the wall had spread and changed in appearance. It now had a shine to it and it seemed to be crawling up the wall.

Hugo was waiting for her when she got to the top of the stairs.

Chapter 10

Garth walked through the door around 7 p.m. with good old dinner standby Chinese in hand. Zoe hadn't felt like cooking. "Baylor said he would be back the first of next week to get the cooler installed," she told him as he set things down on the counter.

Garth was relieved. He didn't want to take more days off to deal with this last loose end in the house renovation saga.

Zoe could tell it'd been a long day for Garth. She pulled him to her and gently massaged his shoulders and neck, and then made little circles at his temples with her fingertips. Eventually, he relaxed and started feeling better.

"Talked to Josh today. If we don't freeze our butts off, we're going to play a round of golf this weekend. You girls want to come along?"

"What's the catch?"

"No catch, just the pleasure of your company."

"Oh, puuleeze. I left my boots downstairs, by the door. Maggie is already talking house hunting."

"Poor guy, I know what he's in for!"

"Oh, stop complaining," Zoe chided. "You know you love this place."

"That I do, woman of the house. I'll be working the next twenty years to pay it off. By the way, did Baylor give you a price for whatever you two figured out?"

"He said he'd have the figures next week. Garth, to be honest, I wish we hadn't even started this project. We haven't been down there in three or four weeks, and I don't even think it would add that much value to the house."

"Don't tell me that," Garth moaned dramatically. "All I heard about for weeks was what a cozy little wine cellar retreat it would be."

"Yeah, you made your point. I just want it to be finished." Then, with mischief in her eyes, she said, "We can talk about Maggie and Josh's wedding and house hunting now, instead."

Garth lowered his head, faking surrender. "You are a cruel, cruel woman, Mrs. Avery."

"You love it!" she beamed. "I'll call Maggie tomorrow, maybe even Rach — she might need a break from the boys. She feels comfortable enough now to leave Lech in charge. Then, it will be three against two."

"Three women and a weekend of golf? I'm sorry I asked."

"You *will* be when I'm done with you."

"I don't take too kindly to threats, ma'am."

"Oh, come on," she coaxed. "Will you let Hugo in? I'm going to I take a shower."

Garth flipped on the patio lights and called Hugo. "Zoe, you know that snake you saw couple days ago? Have you seen anymore?"

"No," she said. "Why do you ask?"

"No reason other than I saw two crossing the driveway when I got the mail, and they weren't small."

Garth knew the other snake had been large, too, because he'd dealt with disposing of the body. He still didn't believe Zoe's wolf story, though. *It had to be a neighborhood dog, like a Husky or Malamute*, he thought, *even though Zoe keeps insisting it was a wolf.*

"It's not like I haven't seen snakes before, it's just unusual to see three in that many days."

Zoe was on her way upstairs as Garth waited patiently for Hugo. The big dog came running when Garth called him, then he closed and locked the door behind him.

Meanwhile, the base of the fountain came alive with pulsating movement, like a slippery heart in a fresh cadaver. And then there were eight.

All the while, the great beast stood watch.

Chapter 11

It was cold and windy, but Zoe took her morning walk anyway. She always felt better after she hit the fresh morning air. The garden's little waterfall brook had started to develop a thin cover of ice, and the fall foliage was quickly removing its curtain of autumn color to reveal the blue spruce and evergreens.

The pine smell loomed heavy and still in the air, and she noticed the morning mist was quickly developing into a cloak of thick and deceptive gray fog. Her clear, cold morning was turning ominous, complete with dark, heavy cloud cover coming to block out the sun.

She could barely see Hugo when a cold shiver prompted her to call to him. He was quickly at her side. "Let's go in, boy. It's getting too dark and cold to be out here."

Once inside, Zoe went to her study and clicked the giant fireplace to life. *Ahh, gas. I love it!* There had always been a large fireplace in all the homes where she'd lived. The dreadful cleanup of wood ash and debris was the pain to the pleasure she got from the fire. *This gas fire is perfect — all the pleasure and none of the mess!*

She called Rachel's house at ten, and Josh answered the phone. "Well, good morning. I expected Rachel to answer. Why are you at your mom's so early?"

"Just thought I'd come out and visit with her and the boys. I think she has plans to talk turkey and mistletoe. This will be the first holiday since she got custody of the boys. I know she wants to make it special for them so they understand this is a whole new chapter in their lives."

"That's wonderful, Josh. Those boys have been the most amazing gift for her."

"Yes, they have."

"I thought she might like to hang out with Maggie and me this weekend while you two are playing golf. *If* you play golf. You're both nuts to play when it's this cold."

"We'll bundle up and it'll be fine. Well, here's Mom," Josh said as he handed over the phone

Lech came roaring down the steps, just as Josh relinquished the phone. Like most teens, he was in a hurry. He had his hat and coat on already and waiting impatiently. He and Josh were going to have some guy time.

Lech had clearly "adopted" Josh as his big brother, and there was no more fear or apprehension on his part. He'd realized there was no reason to hide in the shadows or worry about being separated from his twin brothers.

During the year when Lech and his brothers, Nicolas and Peter, were smuggled from their homeland, they weren't allowed to speak. They were starved, abused, and separated from each other. Lech was even left for dead. It was nothing short of God's miracle that brought them to the attention of Josh Lawton.

It was only in the final days of Nelson R. Beckman's life — a life taken by this abused young man named Lech — that he and Josh crossed paths. Lech killed the evil man to save himself and his brothers. Beckman's death had revealed many dark and unspeakable secrets.

No one had realized the extent of the evil Beckman had perpetrated on those around him. Police and private investigations revealed he was a sinister and vile human being and an abuser of children and flesh peddler. The news articles announcing his death and the subsequent capture of his killer pictured three pathetic, starved babies, and brought Josh squarely into the thick of it.

Removing the children from the authorities and gaining temporary custody did little to alleviate their fears. They refused to speak, and medical examination of the children revealed they'd been subjected to sadistic treatment, including burns, beatings and sexual trauma. This proved to Josh that Beckman was corrupt in mind, body and soul.

The trauma and pain he left behind was almost irreparable. The boys found sanctuary in the love of Josh and his mother, Rachel. A year of love, kindness and nurturing slowly brought the children back from the precipice. Trust did not come easily for them.

Rachel had her parents and sister torn from her and lost to the concentration camps during the Holocaust, so she understood some of what the children were going through. Ironically, it had been

Beckman, the young son of a Gestapo officer, who'd saved her from a similar fate. He bartered for her life, allowing her to escape the death camps.

Rachel had lived with nightmares about that time in her life for years. Because of this, she was prepared for the children's cries in the night and knew how to soothe them. Her loving and patient nature eventually won their hearts and Peter, Nicholas and Lech had learned to smile again.

They weren't the only ones to benefit. The nightmares Rachel had experienced for decades had finally ended, and she was sure the children were responsible for her new lease on life. Saving and adopting them had made her whole again.

Eventually, the courts had legally made them a family, but they all knew they'd become a real family before receiving the legal seal of approval.

Lech would always remember his parents in Romania but his ties to Josh and Rachel would forever be secured.

Josh motioned Lech to the front door so they could leave before Rachel found something else for them to do. She was still on the phone when Josh waved to her and closed the door.

Chapter 12

Rachel decided the fresh air and an outing with the girls would be great. She loved being around the younger women, and she liked that they valued her input on such things as wedding planning, catering and home decor.

Lech was old enough to take care of the other children while she was gone for a few hours. Truth be told, Lech's background and escape from a country filled with killers and tyrants made him more capable than most kids his age. He and his brothers had gotten past being Beckman's victims, and were well on their way to becoming well-rounded young men.

Garth was graciously playing footman and chauffer for the outing. He helped her into her carriage, and she got into the back seat of the Explorer between the two giggling young women. She waved goodbye to the boys, said hello to Josh, who was in the passenger seat, then settled into the girl talk as Garth drove to the golf course.

Zoe got behind the wheel after they dropped off Arnold Palmer and Jack Nicklaus at the bag drop on the golf course. There were a few "hardies" out playing, but most had opted to stay out of the cold.

"We'll be back in about four hours. That should give you Neanderthals enough time to freeze your butts off," Zoe said, then blew a kiss to them both as she took off.

"Okay, girls. Where to?"

Maggie and Rachel both sounded off at once. They'd been conspiring while Zoe was helping the guys with their golf gear.

"It's still a little early, but by the time we get to Frankie's in the village, they'll be open," Rachel said. "We could start off with a hot toddy and a bagel. Starbucks doesn't hold a candle to Frankie's."

So the day began. The girls talked for almost two hours at their table at Frankie's, before heading out the door to hit the stores.

Rachel had a renewed interest in shopping. The arrival of the boys, and Josh's impending wedding had prompted her to update her furnishings and wardrobe.

Evil Entombed

They all stood around the perfume counter at the department store like giggling teens while Rachel picked out a new and exciting scent. Her signature perfume, Chanel No. 5, was falling by the wayside in favor of a younger, fresher scent.

Rachel also decided a new hairstyle was in order. So, while Zoe and Maggie laid waste to Saks Fifth Avenue, Rachel got the works at the salon.

Four hours certainly wasn't enough time for the girls to gossip, shop, and primp! Zoe called the two U.S. Open contenders to let them know they were running late. They were in the bar sipping Jack Daniels to warm up after Josh's crushing defeat by Garth. "How are you boys doing?" she asked sheepishly.

"Okay. Why?"

"Can you two find your way back home on your own? It looks like we're going to be a little longer than we thought."

"Not to worry, we'll both hitch a ride back home with Doc Mellon. We met up with him at the bar, and if we both have any more, we might need him. I'm sure he won't mind."

"That's great, thank him for me. See you tonight. Love you."

53

Garth returned to the bar to announce that the girls had abandoned them. They both turned to Doc Mellon and put their thumbs in the air in a playful pitch for a ride home.

"Sure, boys, sure. What are neighbors for? You two might as well have one more for the road. "You'll need it when the girls' shopping bill comes in."

Chapter 13

Zoe pulled into her driveway about 8 p.m. She and the girls had certainly made a day of it. The Explorer was filled with bags containing new shoes, sweaters, pants and make-up. Rachel had looked great with a new hairstyle, and Maggie had done some shopping for her trousseau.

Zoe was tired, and decided that all the packages could be brought inside later. *I'm not about to do it tonight*, she thought.

When she came in, Garth was asleep on the couch, so she quietly slipped upstairs, kicked her shoes off, shed her clothes, and put on her big fluffy robe. She'd decided to take a nice hot shower in her new bathroom. Tearing out the two walls of the small original bathroom had transformed it to an inviting, updated spa that she just loved.

She removed her robe and casually stepped into her walk-in shower. Before turning on the faucets, she reached for the shampoo, only to feel something large lightly hit her fingertips and scurry over her hand. It fell directly at her feet, and she realized it was a huge spider.

She turned in fear and horror, only to find herself face to face with another arachnid. When a third spider came to join the party, she screamed.

By the time Garth reached the bedroom, she was on her fifth scream, as more spiders danced over the bathroom floor. They were black, hairy and somehow seemed ominous.

Garth started killing them as Zoe frantically fled the room. He killed three others as Zoe sobbed in abject terror.

"It's over," he cooed, while holding her tightly. She was tense and shaking. Several minutes passed before Garth was able to feel her relax.

"My God, where did they come from?" Zoe whispered.

"I don't know,"Garth said, as he managed to free himself from Zoe's grasp. He quickly started removing the uninvited dead guests with large wads of tissue, and then unceremoniously flushed them down the commode.

The spiders' remains left small gobs of white goo everywhere they'd met their demise. Garth cleaned it up with spray cleaner as he said, "Maybe all the construction scared them into the house. They're gone now, so you can take your shower."

"Not tonight I'm not. Not after that."

"Come on, let's go down and sit by the fire." Garth led her to the couch and held her tight as they watched Bruce Willis heroically save hostages held by tyrannical German terrorists in *Die Hard.*

Assured that all was well with the vanquished bad guys, and only after Bruce and his wife faded out in snowy darkness with cheery Christmas music in the background, did they flip the large screen off.

The happy ending didn't help Zoe sleep well. Even with Garth's comforting embrace she had a troubled, fitful sleep filled with dark and heinous images of faceless men on horseback wielding swords and slashing flesh and sinew.

Blood red hands reached out for her as rats scurried around her feet. She awoke with a start.

Garth was up by this time and had opened the blinds to a glorious sunny day. He kissed her lightly on the forehead and told her coffee would be ready when she came downstairs. With that, Garth quickly slipped from the room, with Hugo hot on his heels.

Thank God it's Sunday. That was a terrible night and I don't want to be here alone right now.

Chapter 14

When a sleepy-eyed Zoe found her way down to the kitchen, Garth was looking out the French doors and into the distance. When Zoe poured her coffee, Garth finally realized she was there. "Honey, come here," he said as he turned and motioned her to the window. "Look at that," he whispered as Zoe came close and peered out.

"What am I supposed to be seeing?"

"Hugo. Look at him."

"I see him. What's he doing?"

"Well, don't you see it?"

"See what?" Zoe asked.

Garth looked out confused. "He's gone. Remember, you said you thought you saw a wolf. Well, I could've sworn I saw him out there with Hugo this morning. They were sitting side by side, like they were old chums or something. I've never seen anything like it. Now, just like that, he's gone."

Garth opened the door and called for Hugo, and the big dog came running. He lovingly put his great snout in Zoe's hand and she scratched behind his ear.

"He is such a big baby."

"You know, Garth, he's been acting a little nuts lately. He won't leave my side during the day when you're not here. Come to think of it, it's been going on since that snake incident when he tried to protect me. That's when I first saw the wolf. You think he's back?"

Garth shook his head. "I don't know, I thought you were a little nuts when you told me you saw a wolf. I still think it was probably a neighbor's dog."

Garth stepped outside, and breathed in deeply, enjoying the cool wakeup call to his lungs. Zoe followed, and they both sat briefly until Garth decided he would take a short run up the road before discussing where they needed to put the shed before he ordered it.

They'd decided they needed a large storage shed to store outdoor furniture, flower pots, mowers and garden tools. So many loose ends pop up when moving in a new home, and it seems to take forever to get settled.

Zoe still had a few boxes downstairs that she hadn't unpacked. She'd be glad when Baylor got the wine cooler business resolved. One good thing was the newness of her kitchen hadn't worn off yet. She absently reached for a cookbook as she called out to Garth to ask if he had anything special in mind for dinner.

"Please, no experiments!" he pleaded. "A simple hamburger will do."

"You're just chicken," she called out. "You have no culinary adventure in you."

Garth heard nothing but his own muffled cry as he opened the doors of the dressing area to retrieve his running shoes and sweats and the biggest rat he'd ever seen sneered up at him, its teeth bared.

Even though he'd been on lots of construction sites and had visited Middle Eastern bazaars, he'd never seen a rat this big before. Its beady yellow eyes stared at him with contempt. It wasn't afraid of him and slowly dragged its long, hairless tail over the Notre Dame sweatshirt he'd dropped when he saw the little devil.

It left droppings on the sweatshirt as it disdainfully stared back at him, seeming to dare him to make a move. Garth kept a small caliber .22 in his nightstand for emergencies and protection, and he reached for it now.

This would be a first. Other than target practice, Garth had never shot anything before in his life. He was not a hunter, but he *was* a good shot.

He aimed at the rodent, who finally sensed danger and was making its retreat to the darkness at the back of the closet. He fired, and a high-pitched squeal proved he'd hit his target. The rat gave one last snarl, showing its yellow teeth, then died.

Within seconds, Hugo and Zoe were at Garth's side. Quickly shutting the door to the closet, he sat Zoe down to calm her. "It's nothing. It's all over."

Zoe was not the hysterical type, but she'd heard the gunshot and wanted to know what had happened.

"It was a rat, Zoe. I just killed a rat. A *big* rat, but it's gone now. Maybe you could go down and get the broom and dustpan and a trash bag so I can scoop it up, bag it and get rid of it."

Zoe immediately popped up and quickly returned, broom and bag in hand.

"Go on now, I'll be down in a minute," he said. "I think I'll leave my walk until later. Take Hugo with you when you go downstairs."

Zoe and the dog beat a hasty retreat so Garth could deal with the offending corpse. Minutes later, he came down, went out the back door, and unceremoniously dumped the bag in the large dumpster.

He'd changed into jeans and a flannel shirt with the sleeves rolled up. After disposing of his nasty cargo, he immediately scrubbed from hand to elbow with soap and then bleach.

He sat down with the sigh of a man considering a job well done. *This was not the best beginning to a Sunday morning*, he thought as the looked at the clock. Morning had just about run its course. There would be no more discussion about the uninvited "guest" today, but tomorrow he'd contact a pest control company to do a thorough sweep of the house.

First spiders and now rats, and as Zoe and Garth sat down for the rest of their Sunday afternoon, unbeknownst to them, the walls surrounding them were taking on a life of their own.

Chapter 15

Garth's departure for work had left her feeling optimistic and happy this Monday morning. She was looking forward to Baylor and his contractor coming to analyze the next best step for completing the installation of the monstrous wine cooler.

They were due by 11, which left enough time for her to take Hugo on a morning walk. The sun felt warm and comforting as they both followed the fence line surrounding the property, with Hugo staying noticeably close to her side.

A doe and her two offspring were quietly grazing beyond the fence in the neighboring field. Zoe and Hugo's arrival didn't seem to disturb them. Dog and human watched them quietly until an offending roll of thunder and a cloud shadow seemed to motivate them to leave. There would be no rain today.

The clouds and rumble of thunder were gone just as quickly as they arrived.

Looping their way around behind the giant pines, Zoe had the uncanny feeling that she was being watched, but not in a bad way. Looking behind her, she felt oddly secure and protected. These woods and everything in them seemed to embrace her with a mantle of quiet strength.

As their morning walk came to an end, Hugo was the first to reach the French doors. The big dog bounded inside, followed by Zoe, who immediately felt an unwelcome change in her surroundings.

The temperature in the house had dropped. It felt like she'd walked into a meat locker. Outside, the day was bright and clear, but it was so dim inside that she couldn't see the thermostat in the hall.

She reached for the light switch and heard an annoying click, indicating there was no electricity. "What now?" With a exasperated sigh, she reached for a flashlight in the kitchen drawer, and of course found none.

Garth had strategically placed the power box in the pantry, so she had that to be grateful for. The open kitchen and design of the home let plenty of light filter in, but it was still shadowy. She opened the pantry door and walked right into a sticky, wispy web. It covered her face and bound her arms, causing her to shout out loud in disgust.

With arms flailing and legs desperately backtracking, she fought to get the soft bonds of the web off. In her hurry, she fell backwards, and then scrambled across the floor to the openness of the foyer on her hands and knees.

Her heart beating wildly, she clawed at her face and body trying to remove the sticky threads. Zoe tried to calm herself. She knew it was just a spider web, but she couldn't help the tears.

A knock of the giant lion's head doorknocker announced Tom Baylor's arrival. She got up and ran to answer the door. She'd never been more grateful to see another human being.

Chapter 16

Gathering her wits, Zoe tried her best to appear normal when she opened the door. It didn't work. Tom Baylor knew Zoe well enough to know something was wrong.

"What's going on, Zoe?"

"Oh, nothing really. Just a little power outage."

Tom introduced Ken, his contract foreman, and he shook Zoe's frigid and trembling hand. "Maybe I can take a look around and see what's up."

"Yes, please. I'd appreciate it. The electrical box is in the kitchen. Please be careful." Ken already knew where it was, since he'd worked with Garth early in the renovation.

While Ken went to check things out, Tom motioned Zoe to her easy chair and covered her with a nearby blanket once she sat down. He then found the remote for the fireplace and clicked it on.

About that time, the house filled with light and the furnace kicked on.

Ken came in, smiling. "That better?"

"Much, much better! Thank you."

"What happened here?"

Both men sat down and listened intently as she explained. Zoe had regained her composure and was able to communicate the silliness of the whole thing.

"It was dark and cold, and I ran into something in the pantry. It gave me a fright, that's all. I'm feeling better now. Can I make you gentlemen some coffee?"

"No, we're fine. Why don't we take a look downstairs? I want Ken to see what he thinks we're dealing with. He's going to check that hole, the integrity of the walls, and check out the ground around it, so we can finish this project."

"You don't know how happy that makes me." Zoe beamed. "I've started to hate that hole and even the idea of the wine cooler being down there. It seemed like a great idea at the time, but now I'm not so sure. What's worse, now Garth won't let me live it down. I don't even like to go down there."

Ken went out to his truck for his equipment, and came back with a ladder, hardhat, tool belt and tool bag. He carefully maneuvered the ladder down the stairs and Tom followed. Zoe left them to their work.

Both men stared into the hole. "This is a 50-foot ladder, it should do it, but I brought a harness, too, just in case we need it."

Tom looked at Ken and grinned. "I'm glad you're the one going down there and not me."

The well easily swallowed the 50-foot ladder, and the end just touched what seemed to be solid ground. Ken rigged up a rope for the descent, just to be safe, and put on his hardhat with the light on top. "Damn! It's creepy and cold down here," he said as he started the descent.

As he slowly climbed down, he noticed the same black ooze that covered the north wall, was even thicker on the walls as he went down. The width of the hole remained the same for perhaps 10 feet, and then abruptly widened to cave-like area that looked more natural than manmade. The black ooze was here, too.

Ken's good humor abruptly left him as he continued his subterranean adventure. He was cold and at the same time sweating. He usually wasn't afraid of confined spaces, but this one was making him uncomfortable.

He'd been in more difficult surroundings during his career, but this was different. Fear gripped his heart and he began to tremble. He heard Tom's reassuring voice asking if everything was okay. Getting ahold of himself, he answered, "I think I'm almost to the bottom."

Shining the light below, he saw that was indeed the case. His boots found purchase on a smooth set of boulders covered in water seepage and muck. His light showed the contour of the floor and the walls of the well. The walls seemed solid, with no crumbling areas or fallen rock.

As he swung his light around, it picked up a reflection, blinding Ken for a moment. When he could see again, he came face to face with every little boy's nightmare — a grinning skull hanging loosely from connecting bones. It was leering at him as he backpedaled.

His heart came to a momentary stop. He climbed back on the bottom rung of the ladder and yelled up at Tom that he was coming up.

When he got to the top, he breathlessly said, "Scared the shit out of me!"

"What?"

"A freakin' skeleton. Never expected to find something like that down there! We'd better tell Mrs. Avery that she has an uninvited guest."

Shakily, Ken removed his boots, cleaned himself up and quickly followed Tom up the stairs. "I don't believe this."

After the two explained what Ken found, Zoe said, "Most people will never deal with one skeleton in a lifetime, I've had to deal with dozens." Her mind immediately went to the remains of the children the company uncovered on a jobsite last year. It had quickly turned into a crime scene and media circus tied to Beckman's death.

"Garth is never going to believe this," she added as she reluctantly picked up the phone.

By the time Garth got home, local police cars were parked around the circular driveway. Zoe's dream house had taken on the aura of a bad dream.

As he walked through the door, Garth heard several voices down in the cellar. Zoe hadn't wanted to go down there, so she was sitting at the counter with Hugo by her side.

Looking at Garth, she said, "Remember when you called this the house from hell? I'm beginning to agree with you."

Garth acknowledged that statement and then joined the others in the cellar. The officers were busily taking statements and roping off the area. After all the questions were answered, the officer in charge thought removal of the "evidence" would best be done with the proper equipment and personnel.

He told Garth they would have people there early the next day to remove and tag the remains properly. He thanked them for their cooperation and left.

Tom and Ken decided they were done for the day, even though the wine cooler situation was unresolved.

Zoe found she could no longer laugh about the "little" setbacks in the completion of her home.

"Come on, Zoe. Let's go to the Village and shake off some of this gloom," Garth said after everyone had left..

Zoe threw on a coat, and they were out the door.

By the time they returned, both were in better spirits.

"Are we really going to sleep here tonight with that thing in the cellar?" she asked.

"Don't worry, honey. If the boogeyman comes, I'll protect you."

They both chuckled, as Garth snuggled up close to Zoe and held her tight.

As they slept, Hugo kept watch. Curled up by the door, he listened intently for the cry of the wolf.

Chapter 17

Between the time our Continental troops were being routed by the British, Washington crossed the Delaware to capture the Hessians at Trenton, and General John Burgoyne's British forces took Ticonderoga in Philadelphia, Col. Cecil Bradford flourished. He was one of the most hated men in the King's army. He managed to survive all battles — not for God or Country, home or hearth, but for the joy of killing. He loved it. He drew power from it.

Needless to say, his superiors never called Col. Bradford a hero. They knew he had an insatiable bloodlust. His was notorious for his cruelty, and his rumors of his treachery had reached the ears of the colonists.

Hangings were routine for him, as were destruction of crops and livestock. These were his diversions.

The battle of Long Island was his final battle. Fate being what it is, and being accountable to none, we find the evil spirit of Col. Bradford, who was killed by the wolf on a day in 1775, awakened when the well was uncovered and his remains were found.

Col. Bradford had quietly slipped into Zoe's nightmare this night. She heard herself screaming as she awoke on sweat-soaked sheets. Garth reached for her and held her tight, murmuring, "It's okay. Everything's okay. Wake up, baby. It's just a bad dream."

He turned the light on and was alarmed by the look of terror on her face. She was white as a sheet and breathing heavily.

"I felt a cold blade at my throat," she whispered breathlessly. "My hands were slippery with blood, and I saw a sea of marching men dressed in red."

Garth's reassuring cooing and loving embrace began to quiet her. When he felt it was safe to release her, he went downstairs to get her a good stiff drink. Since, Zoe didn't like taking pills, this was the ony thing he could think of to help settle her nerves.

When he returned, he found she'd showered, changed her pajamas, and was somewhat recovered. "Here, drink this."

"Oh, this should do it. I'm already feeling much better after showering. I don't know what's wrong with me. I usually don't dream, much less have nightmares. We didn't have anything strange for dinner like sauerkraut and sausage, did we?" She laughed.

"Come back to bed. You've even upset the dog."

She patted the Hugo's head, and got into bed.

"I could almost swear that Hugo was in my dream. Maybe, when all this uproar dies down, we can get back to normal. How in God's name do we get tangled up in these messes? I'll bet we're the only family in Long Island that discovered anything like that in their cellar."

"Well, Zoe, you can't say this house hasn't been full of surprises. *And*, might I remind you, you were the one that just *had* to have this house," he said with a flutter of his eyelashes and an exaggerated sigh. "Come on, back to bed. Let's get some sleep. I'm sure the authorities will be here early tomorrow to take care of everything."

Zoe snuggled close to Garth and slept soundly the rest of the night. Hugo kept watch.

Chapter 18

By 9 a.m., the Avery household was teaming with the local Suffolk police — hazmat suits and all. Trained forensics officers and looky lous surrounded the place. Local gossip had already spread through the village, and everyone was talking about the skeleton in the well.

Zoe made pots of steaming coffee and asked Maggie to bring over donuts and sweet rolls for the detectives and officers. Garth had also called Josh, who said he'd be right over. By the time he arrived, the curiosity seekers had been herded away from the house by the officers.

As Suffolk ambulance and coroner were awaiting the remains, three of the officers in hazmat suits found themselves at the bottom of the well, discussing the most expedient and safe way to disengage the fleshless intruder.

The team had also found bits of leather, metal, and other disintegrating materials and rotting fibers. They were all bagged and tagged so further examination could be made. The entire skeleton and the surrounding residue were gently placed in a short-sided square box and sent up via a pulley to officers above.

Then, a team of two women dressed in white coveralls and gloves took over, bagging and tagging every tidbit they could find. Obviously, Col. Bradford received far more respectful treatment in the 20th century than he had during his lifetime.

In the meantime, the neighbors descended on the home and Zoe and Garth found themselves meeting them under unusual circumstances. Maggie had luckily brought enough refreshments for everyone. Zoe found out some of them were just as curious about the old house as they were about the discovery in the cellar. They all said they were thrilled by the home's transformation.

Rachel eventually found her way over, too. She came bearing freshly baked cupcakes and cinnamon rolls. One resident in particular had come to see Zoe after she heard about the discovery. Mrs. Pangborn, a distinguished lady in her late seventies, had a nodding acquaintance with Rachel.

Rachel told her how good it was to see her doing well, since she'd been ill health previously.

"Good to see you, too, Rachel. Curiosity brings me out. What did they find?"

"Come on, I'll introduce you to Zoe. She's the one that decided to renovate this White Elephant. She can tell you all about it."

The forensic team and detectives finished up around 1:30 p.m. They all seemed nonplussed about the whole situation, since this could not officially be called a crime scene. They partook of the refreshments, too, before finally gathering up all of their paraphernalia and heading out.

This left Zoe, Garth, Josh, Maggie, Rachel and a few stranglers from the community. Garth, Zoe and Maggie all played gracious hosts for the next 30 minutes, while Rachel and Josh caught up on community news. They finally thanked everyone for coming, telling them how happy they were to meet their new neighbors, and said goodbye.

Mrs. Pangborn hung back to talk to Zoe and Garth. Her interest was the history of the house and the things found in the cellar. She was president of the Suffolk County Historical Society and curator of the small museum housing artifacts from early New England history.

"I knew the owners of this home about 50 years ago," Mrs. Pangborn said. "She and her husband moved here as newlyweds, and I talked to them about the history of the house. I remember sitting in front of the giant fireplace I'm looking at now and listening to the old fellow recount bloodcurdling tales of Indians, and the great battles between the British, French and Americans."

Mrs. Pangborn couldn't remember the man's name, but she certainly remembered his colorful tales and stories of the Red Coats, Cornwallis, and Burgoyne.

"The old gentleman was proud to add that his great-great-grandfather served with Washington. All of the tales were passed down to him by relatives. They were mostly about the early settlement of New York and the surrounding area." Mrs. Pangborn remembered those tales fondly; along with the people she had lost touch with so many years ago. She was a local history buff and that fit right in with her present position.

"You've done a beautiful job with this home," she said. "Its transformation is amazing." She turned wistfully to the fireplace and remarked how beautifully it was preserved after all these years. "I hope you don't mind my reminiscing. It's been a pleasure. I would love it if you'd contact me when you get the results on the items they retrieved today."

"I'd be happy to, Mrs. Pangborn."

"Please, call me Carol."

"Anything I can do to be helpful or contribute to our community, I'd consider it an honor."

Rachel and Mrs. Pangborn decided to leave together, and Zoe hugged Rachel and saw them both to the door.

Josh walked them out to the car and kissed his mother goodbye before going back to the much quieter house. He looked at Maggie, Zoe and Garth, and they all seemed to sigh collectively. "What's next? Chablis or Bordeaux?"

Chapter 19

Zoe had another restless night. She was unable to shake the feeling of dread. When she awoke, Garth was already up. Coffee in hand, he was ready to leave for the office. He had a pile of messages Mrs. Potter said he had to answer.

"What day is it? I've lost track of time since this all began," she mumbled, sleepily.

"Tuesday," he said as he kissed her and prepared leave. "Call Baylor again and update him about the cellar and our 'visitor' being removed. Maybe we can get this thing done."

"If I never hear the word wine cooler again, it will be too soon."

"Me, too."

"Better get to the office before Mrs. Potter sends the dogs out," she said as he left the room.

Pulling herself out of bed, Zoe dressed and went downstairs. She was ready for her morning walk with Hugo. She always felt better after a walk. Once outside, she found it was a chilly morning, filled with the crisp sound of rustling leaves and angry squirrels.

The hairs on the back of her neck suddenly stood on end. There it was again, that uncanny feeling of someone watching her. There was no fear attached to the feeling — it was more like comfort and security surrounding her like a warm blanket. *I feel protected!* The dread and uneasiness she'd felt since waking up suddenly evaporated.

After her walk, she felt refreshed, and she and Hugo headed toward the house so she could call Baylor and make the appointment to finally install the wine cooler. She went to the French doors and turned the knob, but it seemed to be stuck. *What the heck? I didn't lock it when I left, and these doors are certainly too new to be stuck.*

Zoe tried again and pulled hard. The doors balked, but finally opened with a moan like a woman giving birth. It was unnerving. The doors didn't want to cooperate when she closed them, either. Turning the lock, anger engulfed her, and she muttered, "It's this house. Something evil is here."

Hugo came to her, ignoring her agitation, and indicated his bowl was empty with a soft whine. "Sorry, Hugo. I'm starting to have a bad day."

She went to the pantry, opened the door and switched on the light. She reached for the scoop in the 50 pound bag of dog food and screamed as thousands of tiny black insects crawled up her arm and under her sweater. They quickly found their way to her face and scampered through her hair, covering her entire body.

She ran, screaming, with her eyes closed and arms flailing violently as she tried to remove the onslaught. She fearfully felt her way to the bathroom and jumped into the shower, fully clothed. She turned the water on, shucked her clothes and doused herself with soap, as the hot water beat down on her.

She scrubbed and clawed at the invading pests, her tears evaporating in the steam. Barely clinging to her sanity, she got out of the shower and quickly threw on a different set of clothes. Then, she grabbed her keys and made her way back downstairs, calling for Hugo as she went.

Moments later, her SUV raced from the driveway. Rachel was going to have a surprise visitor.

Chapter 20

A while later, Garth joined her at Rachel's. "There's something in that house!" Zoe wailed. "I am *not* crazy." Garth was shushing and holding her like a fretting infant. "You saw those things at the house or you wouldn't be here!"

"I made a call and a pest control team will be there tomorrow."

"It's more than that, Garth. There's something very wrong. I *feel* it in the house. It's like I'm living in a Stephen King novel."

Rachel had called Josh when a shaken Zoe arrived on her doorstep, and Josh had immediately called Garth and told him to head home.

Rachel had sent the boys out back to play with Hugo while she poured Zoe a brandy and calmed her down.

After Zoe calmed down, Garth went home to deal with the bugs and clean up. He hoped they wouldn't put in a repeat performance before the pest control guys showed up.

After that, he decided to work from home rather than return to his office. *Mrs. Potter will just have to change my appointments again,* he thought. *At least Norm has everything under control on the jobsite.*

Before dealing with work, Garth focused on the problems plaguing his new home. *Zoe is right, this is more than an infestation of bugs, snakes and spiders — there are also the nightmares and all the weird stuff going on in the basement. What can be causing it?*

Garth decided to get a full inspection of the house. Knowing how much Zoe loved it, he wanted to put to rest any more fears of infestation or unexpected discoveries.

That decided, he called Baylor and told him he wanted the wine cooler installed by the end of the week, no matter what. He also decided to call the local authorities to see if there would be any problem with continuing the work in the cellar.

When that was done, he headed back to Rachel's house.

"Garth, Zoe can stay here until you get things resolved, if she wants to."

"Honey?" Garth turned to Zoe.

"I'd love that, Rachel, if you're sure it wouldn't be an imposition."

"Not at all, I've got plenty of room. Now go on, Garth, she's in good hands. Do what you have to do."

Garth hugged Zoe and Rachel. "I'll be just down the road if you need me."

After Garth left, Rachel told Zoe that hearing about the day's events had made her remember something from when she and her husband moved to the area some 40 years ago. "There was a couple who lived in your house for several years," Rachel remembered, "but they moved for some reason and it was vacant again.

"After that, it had several owners, but none of them stayed too long. Sounds like maybe that house just has a case of bad karma."

"Oh, I hope that's not true! I love that house," Zoe said defiantly defending the old place. "Besides, I don't believe in bad karma."

"Well maybe you're right. It's not that I believe in karma, exactly. But, I don't disbelieve, either. I can't discount things I don't understand.

"Maybe we should take a ride into the Village tomorrow and visit Mrs. Pangborn at the museum. I'm sure she'll know more about the old place."

"I'd love to do that. I have yet to see all there is to see in our new community."

"Good, the kids will be in school, and I hear there's a new restaurant in town. Lunch is on me. Now, let's make some lunch for the boys, and I'm sure we can find some leftovers for Hugo, too."

Zoe was looking forward to an outing with Rachel. With all the conversation, she'd all but forgotten her terrifying morning.

Chapter 21

Garth finished up some long-ignored paper-work and nailed down orders for new projects that were in the pipeline. He then called Josh regarding petty litigious issues, new contracts and his position with the local authorities about the "infernal hole" he had below his house. He also explained the mess he had on his hands with the bugs and Zoe's growing fear of "something" being in their house.

Josh had spoken to the authorities, and assured Garth he was once again king of his castle. "They've determined the remains are an 'antiquities discovery' and that any foul play involving the deceased happened over 200 years ago. Judging from what little clothing remained, your uninvited visitor dates back to the Revolutionary War.

"You, my friend, are now the proud owner of what seems to be a historical landmark. The fellow they found belongs to you, barring any family member showing up to claim the body." Josh was enjoying this.

"Ha-ha! Okay, I hope Maggie finds a place that gives you a headache just like mine. By the way, Zoe is at your mom's place until the pest control guys give the all-clear. I'm picking her up tomorrow. It's weird. Zoe doesn't usually let things rattle her like this."

"Zoe will be just fine, Garth. The move and living in the middle of a major renovation have probably just gotten to her finally. Don't worry about her. We'll touch base tomorrow."

After Josh hung up, Garth felt like he was sitting in an isolated void. He realized he was surrounded by a vast, dark silence illuminated by just one lonely desk lamp. He missed Zoe and Hugo.

"Make a note, put outside lights on a timer ASAP," he muttered to himself as he made his way to the kitchen through the carpet of black bugs. He grabbed a couple of beers, cheese, crackers, and cold cuts and retreated from the bugs up the stairs. *Hope there's a good movie on tonight.*

After he ate, he called Zoe to remind her everything would be all right, that he loved her, and that she shouldn't worry about anything. He realized his words were hollow comfort when he was surrounded by the unsettling quiet of the house.

He was uneasy and unable to sleep when he went to bed. He usually only got this way when a tough job was dogging him, but tonight was different, and decidedly creepy. His mouth was dry, and he felt feverish.

A John Wayne movie played in the background as Garth got up and paced in front of the window. *I definitely need to install those exterior lights*, he thought as he looked at the inky darkness outside. *It probably wouldn't hurt to install some security measures, too.*

At 2 a.m., he had yet to close his eyes. His brow was sweaty, and he was unable to shake the feeling of dread stalking him. It reminded him of what Zoe had told him when she'd had the flu last month. "Have to get some sleep," he muttered as he grabbed some Advil PM from Zoe's nightstand.

By 3 a.m., Garth had finally managed to drift off to sleep, just as the John Wayne marathon came to an end and The Duke was dragging Maureen O'Hara over the Irish hillside.

As soon as he fell asleep, gray clouds engulfed him in his dream, and he found himself standing in a field surrounded by the screams of men dying in a storm of blood and mud. Unknown hands reached out to him, pleading for mercy. He tried, but failed to reach the cries. The rain-soaked earth crumbled beneath him, swallowing him as he fell into a pool of carnage and darkness.

"Can't get out! Can't get out!" he screamed, scrambling for footing in the airless abyss of death and decay. He was falling, falling ... then suddenly he sat bolt upright, breathing heavily.

Morning cannot come soon enough! he thought as he fell back onto his pillow.

Chapter 22

Garth awoke to bright sunlight filtering through the bedroom widows. The morning presented him with clarity of mind and a resolve to get whatever pests, problems, and loose ends connected with the house renovation behind him. Last night had been particularly unsettling, but the light of day chased away some of the uneasiness.

Garth felt refreshed and ready to face the day. *We're going to get rid of the damned bugs, get the wine cooler set, and be done with it!* he thought as he jumped into the shower. *Bug men first, then Baylor should be here to deal with the cooler.*

Half running down the stairs, he found the house was filled with sunlight, a good accompaniment to his morning coffee. The aroma of coffee and the warmth of his home was comforting this morning.

As he took his first sip of coffee, he looked out through the French doors and paused. There was a large dog sitting on the stone patio, sentry style. *Hugo's with Zoe*, Garth thought, as he slowly walked to the door to look at the animal.

He seemed to know he was being observed, and turned to look at him. There was no fear on either side, as the blue-eyed giant locked eyes with Garth. They stood appraising each other for a bit, and a feeling of serenity settled over man and beast.

Then, the canine turned, looked back for a moment, and trotted toward the hillside at the edge of the property. "That was the most amazing thing I've ever seen. I just came face to face with Zoe's wolf," he said with wonder. "That certainly wasn't a neighbor's dog."

He sat down, mesmerized by what he had just experienced. The feeling of wellbeing the animal had instilled in him remained. He phoned Zoe and told her about his incredible experience, as well as his unsettling dreams of death and terror.

"I'm happy you believe me now, Garth, but I'm sorry you had such an awful night. I knew you didn't really believe me before and were just humoring me. I love our house so much, I just wish all the creepy stuff would stop happening."

"Don't worry, we'll get the kinks worked out. The exterminators should be here sometime this morning, and I'm talking to Baylor this afternoon to hopefully finish up with the cooler.

"Oh, and by the way you are now the proud owner of a historical landmark. I talked to Josh yesterday, and our visitor from below seems to date back to the Revolutionary War. Next thing you know, we might find out that George Washington slept here. We could always charge admission."

Zoe chuckled. "I knew we would find fame and fortune some day. Did I tell you that Rachel's taking me into town today? We're going to visit the town's museum and talk to the curator, Mrs. Pangborn, to see if she knows anything about the history of our house. She was there when the police showed up. Remember?"

"I do. Sounds like you're going to have an interesting day. Hey, looks like the pest control guys are here. This place is going to be de-bugged and sanitized from top to bottom in no time. Enjoy your day. I'll talk to you later. Love you."

When Garth opened the door, he was met by what looked like a bad B-grade movie cast from the '50s. They were dressed top to bottom in hazmat suits, and were armed with spray cans, vacuums and tarps. The one who seemed to be their fearless leader removed his mask, introduced himself and announced they should be done by noon.

Garth let them in and made sure they had everything they needed from him before taking his leave. As he drove down the driveway, he could only wonder how many people had men in hazmat suits crawling all over their house twice in less than a month. *Everything associated with this house is weird, just plain weird.*

Chapter 23

Zoe and Rachel left about 11 a.m. and found themselves at the new restaurant in town, a lovely little teahouse called Imogene's. It served a light fare of salads, soups and sandwiches with the crusts removed, along with magnificent desserts. There was also a tiny shop filled with shiny geegaws, special perfumes and accessories to maneuver through. It was like a field filled with female landmines.

A scarf of intricate Belgian lace caught Zoe's eye as they moved through the shop. She failed to escape its allure, and Rachel found her undoing in a tiny silk beaded bag studded with emerald cut stones set in the design of a Bird of Paradise. Both women left the restaurant with the satisfaction that only shopping therapy can provide.

The two were so elated with their finds that they almost forgot their museum field trip. Rachel had called Mrs. Pangborn earlier to see if she would be at the museum and found out it was only open at certain times throughout the week. They'd been lucky to choose a day when the curator would be there.

The girls quickly made their way over to a small cottage that functioned as the town's historical center. Mrs. Pangborn eagerly greeted them at the door, anxious to share her knowledge of the town's history. She immediately assumed her tour guide persona, showing off muskets, butter churns, and other historical bits and baubles.

There were also mannequins dressed in the attire of the day, including soldiers' uniforms complete with three-cornered hats. There were all manner of books handed down or rescued from someone's attic, beautiful swords, and pistols that were obviously British — the colonies and young patriots hadn't had anything quite so fine.

Personal letters from families and loved ones in England to the colonies were also included. This correspondence was all lovingly preserved and displayed. Personal belongings, like a hanky, tobacco pouch, and coins, had also found a place in Mrs. Pangborn's museum.

As informative as the tour was, Zoe was more interested in learning about her home. "Mrs. Pangborn?"

"Carol, please."

"Carol, do you remember anything unusual or noteworthy about our home?"

"Nothing in particular that I can recall, but I do remember the old fella that lived here telling stories about the Redcoats, bloodthirsty battles and the hangings that came with them. Cyrus, that was his name. His grandfather told him how the British just burst through his door as big as you please and announced they were confiscating his home.

"The general decided his troops were going to be headquartered there. They took all the grain, and livestock, too. Cyrus's ancestors objected and were imprisoned. The General was ordered to move to Brooklyn to quell other uprisings about a month later. He left Col. Cecil Bradford behind to command in his place. Shortly thereafter, Cyrus's ancestors were hung."

"I think one of the letters in that case over there mentions the Colonel," Carol said. "He was referred to as a man without a soul, with eyes of blue that were forged in hatred."

"Also, the sword you see over there belonged to Cyrus. He sold it to me when he moved out of the area. It was one of the first pieces in our little museum."

Carol led Rachel and Zoe to a display case filled with several time-worn Revolutionary War era letters from local families.

Zoe saw the letter Carol was talking about. The old letters and documents were a testament to United States history, as well as the early settlers of Long Island. They'd suffered greatly, not just from the inevitable destruction of war.

Zoe read the thoughts of a young girl, Prudence, who'd written this ominous line in her diary all those years ago, "A thick maelstrom of evil has infected us all in the form of the British soldier, Col. Bradford." Zoe felt a cold shiver run down her spine as she read the faded ink, and lost all curiosity about the remaining antiques.

She thanked Carol for the tour and history lesson, then reminded Rachel that she needed to get back to check on her house. She hoped all remnants of vermin and pests had been eradicated.

Josh and Maggie greeted them when they got back to Rachel's. They'd dropped by for a visit, and, of course, to check on the "House from Hell."

Zoe shot an disapproving glance at Josh when he mentioned that, and said, "I know, I know, you told me the place would be nothing but headaches. I wish that's all it was. I'm beginning to believe in Ichabod Crane, the headless horseman and the Amityville Horror."

Her phone rang, interrupting her tirade. It was Garth, announcing that all vermin, bugs, and bad mojo had been cleared out. "The infernal cooler will be installed by the end of the week," Garth added. "That should put the finishing touches on your dream home.

"We will, of course, have to figure out what to do with our uninvited guest — you know our historical landmark discovery. The locals are done with him, now it's up to us to decide what to do with him. Josh can tell you all about that."

"Josh and Maggie are here now."

"Well good, he can fill you in on our unwanted guest. I'll be there about seven to pick you up."

"My car's here. I can drive myself and Hugo, home in a bit. I'll stop and get us a bite to eat, too."

Josh filled her in on the details about the skeleton and the various other things found with it. Zoe now owned it and all of the rest of the historical junk.

"Ewww! Just get rid of it. I want nothing to do with it!"

"Now, think about this, Zoe," Josh said quickly assuming his head counsel advisory tone. "You may've found some valuable historical artifacts. You could sell them on eBay or something. Just retrieve them from the authorities and then decide what to do within them later."

"All right, Josh. I'll think about it and we can we can talk about it more tomorrow." With that she turned to Maggie and Rachel, hugged them both, said goodbye to the boys and called Hugo who was lying patiently by the fire. Josh walked her out and helped Hugo into the car.

"Everything is going to work out fine," Josh told her.

"I know, Josh. I was just hoping to be settled in before Thanksgiving. I'm looking forward to our holidays there. I'm also looking forward to your mom's pecan pie."

Josh grinned, tapped the door lightly to see her on her way and went quickly back into the house.

"What do you say, Hugo, should we pick up some burgers in the village for your dad?" Zoe asked.

Hugo's ears came to attention, and he answered with a low woof.

"That's what I thought."

Garth had left the porch light on for them, and her home looked warm and welcoming as she drove into the big circular driveway. Garth met her at the front door and kissed her warmly. As he helped her with the take-out, they both failed to notice a low hissing sound emanating from the surrounding woods, but Hugo didn't. He stopped briefly and growled, before hurrying inside with the humans. The big dog would not sleep tonight.

Chapter 24

The morning was bright, clear, and cold, and the wolf was in the clearing, just beyond the wooded area. He was alert and on point. The cold night's vigil made him grateful for the morning sun on his back. He was worn, tired and hungry, but the arrival of daybreak brought him a sense of relief.

He allowed himself a brief rest and lay down in the sun, but didn't close his ancient blue eyes. Evil, as the wolf knew only too well, survives and gains strength by night. The bright sun of the day would keep the growing entity at bay for the time being.

The French doors of the home opened, and the man-dog bounded out. Both humans looked out and saw the wolf as he lay resting.

"Look, Garth, he's here again."

They both stared in amazement as Hugo approached the wolf like he was a long-lost brother and lay down beside him. The woods had come alive with squirrels, birds, frogs, chipmunks and all manner of creatures stirring to life with the sun.

Zoe refilled their mugs with strong black coffee and quickly started a fresh pot. "I noticed you didn't sleep very well," she mused. "You tossed all night. You've done that the past several nights. It's been that way for me, too. I slept great at Rachel's, though."

They both looked tired as they peered out the window and marveled at the new friendship between their dog and the mysterious wolf. They instinctively knew the animal meant no harm. "Garth, do you think we should call someone about it?"

"What for? He's not bothering anything. Actually it's a comfort to have him around."

"I can't believe you said that. But, I know what you mean. How do you know it's a he?"

Garth was halfway up the stairs as he answered. "I don't know. That's just the impression I got. I'm going to get dressed. Remember, you've got me all day today. Baylor should be here with his men to install the cooler, too."

"Great, that job can't be done soon enough!"

The warmth of the sun poured through the window, luring Zoe outside. So, she followed Garth upstairs to get dressed. A long walk on this warm November day was just what she needed to lift her spirits. She pulled on her favorite pair of jeans, a cozy old sweater and a pair of L.L. Bean boots.

When they went downstairs, Garth went to his office to check his messages, while Zoe checked for leftovers in the fridge. She found a large portion of sirloin tip to offer Hugo's new friend.

Her enthusiasm for an early morning walk quickly came to an end as she opened the door to find Hugo barring her way, and the wolf standing near the patio stairs. She initially thought he just wanted to play, but quickly changed her mind when he jumped on her and pushed her back towards the door. It was then that she noticed the dead, sand-colored snake at the end of the flagstone.

As she looked up, she saw another dead snake splayed in the grass. As she started looking around the yard, she saw another and another and yet another. Horrified, she stepped back into the house and quickly closed the door, leaving Hugo and the wolf outside.

"GARTH!" she screamed, his name reverberating throughout the house. She didn't move until he was there, standing beside her. She leaned against him, shaking and sobbing. "It's this house, damn it! I know it's this house."

"Calm down. What's going on?"

"Look. Just look outside."

Stepping out in the clear, bright day, Garth didn't immediately see anything amiss, other than the steak Zoe had dropped. Hugo barked, and Garth looked in the dog's direction.

What he saw shocked him. There were a multitude of serpent intruders. Most were dead, but some were still thrashing around. The color drained from Garth's face. *This is not good,* he thought as he came back inside and closed the door.

It was only 9:30 in the morning, but Zoe had poured herself a good two ounces of whiskey and had finished half of it by the time Garth came back in. He hugged her tightly and assured her everything would be all right.

"But it's not," she wailed, "and it just keeps getting worse!"

"Shh! We will figure this out," Garth tried to reassure her in his most take-charge voice, but by this time they both understood something truly strange was going on.

The there was a knock at the door, and Garth went to answer it. It was Baylor. *At least he can deal with one of our problems*, Garth thought as he let him inside. *Too bad a new, more troubling one just surfaced.* Baylor's men followed him inside, and they went right to work.

While Garth dealt with the construction crew, Zoe refilled her mug with coffee, laced it with more whiskey, and grabbed her laptop to retreat upstairs. The feeling of dread surrounding her and grabbing her by the throat was slowly being replaced by a deep-seated anger.

To distract herself, she called Maggie for a smidgen of girl talk and to find out latest on her house hunting expeditions. "It does get confusing," Zoe agreed when Maggie commented on how difficult it was to decide on a home. "I really thought you'd just *know* when you saw it."

"Hey," Maggie exclaimed, "I'm meeting Josh later this afternoon. How about I come earlier, say about two? We can have a late lunch in the village and talk."

"Sounds like a perfect plan to me. Garth is here to deal with the workmen finishing up with the wine cooler. Getting out of here sounds great. There's just too much bad mojo going on around here for me. I'll see you in a bit."

After she disconnected the call, she muttered, "Bad mojo, that's all it is. Can't see it but I know it's there," she mumbled. "Something has changed in this house."

What was really getting her down was knowing that at first sight she'd known this place was hers, that feeling had been replaced by a feeling of fore-boding. Lying across the bed, she Googled "paranormal infestations" and "evil spirits." She was determined to educate herself.

After reading up on all sorts of things, she decided to give Father Fitzhugh a call. He hadn't seen her new home, and she hadn't spoken to him since they started the renovations. *I know, I'll call him tomorrow and invite him to Thanksgiving at Rachel's. That will be perfect. While he's there, I'll ask him to come by and bless the house.* Zoe felt she needed his guidance and spiritual counsel.

The idea of having their home blessed made her feel better. There was no doubt in her mind now — she was certain she was surrounded by evil and it had invaded her home.

While Zoe was having her epiphany, Baylor and his men nervously worked on covering and sealing the old well, before doing the wiring for the wine cooler and setting it place. None of them could figure out why they were so uneasy, but they all knew they wanted to get the job done and get out of the creepy cellar.

Hugo and the wolf remained on sentry duty out side the entire time.

Chapter 25

G arth made a quick trip to the village while the crew worked on the cooler. When he returned, he was armed with gasoline, thick gloves, heavy-duty trash bags, and trashcans. He gathered the offending serpents surrounding the patio, piled them up and soaked them in gasoline before setting them on fire. Garth stood by with the hose just in case, and watched the pyre burn, repulsed. By the time only ashes were left, he was shaking and his blood ran cold. *Zoe is right. Evil has come to visit us.*

After he finished, he took off his jacket. The fire and the sickening sight and smell of this cleanup were making him sweat. He then went in the house and got a glass of ice-cold water and drank it down.

When he finished, he yelled down to Baylor and asked him to come up to talk. The sound of screeching metal on metal and concrete guns made him hope this nightmare project would soon be over.

Baylor met Garth at the top of the stairs. At Garth's suggestion, they went into the kitchen and he poured himself a cup of coffee, before they sat down at the counter to discuss the progress.

They were friends and had worked together on many projects over the years. The men were about the same age, and Baylor had worked for Zoe's father as a subcontractor when he was younger — about the time Garth joined the company.

The two shared a few beers every so often, and they'd both tackled some almost impossible jobs over the years. This was the first time Garth had every seen Baylor back off on a job. He was not a meek man, but today he looked pale and uneasy. Garth also noticed him using the word "creepy" more than once.

"My men can't wait to get out of here," Baylor blurted.

Garth was surprised that something could rattle his big, burley friend. "I know *exactly* what you're talking about," Garth said. They'd known each other too long for deception.

Baylor finished his coffee, happy he'd passed his feelings on to Garth, but even happier this job would be completed by day's end. "Oh, by the way, that creepy black ooze keeps coming back. We'll give it one more scrub-down on final cleanup, but I won't guarantee it will stay gone. Once that's done, we're out of here," he said, his voice fading as he disappeared down the steps.

"Can't say I blame you," Garth muttered to himself, as he turned his attention to the French doors. Hugo was standing there, waiting to be let in. He hadn't come in last night because he wouldn't leave his new friend.

Garth opened the door and the big dog went directly to his bowl, hungrily "wolfed" down his food, and then lapped up some water, leaving giant puddles on the floor. When he was done, he immediately went to the door to be let back out. "Just in on a break, are we?" Garth asked him.

The big dog's ears perked up and he looked at him inquiringly. "Okay. What is it you want? Oh, your buddy needs some kibble, too, you say?

"Not so sure it's his cup of tea, but we'll see what we can do."

113

Garth retrieved a large container, filled it with dog food and threw in a few odds and ends from the refrigerator. He let Hugo out and followed him to the edge of the patio and down the steps, where he set the food down. He also grabbed a bucket and filled it with water from the hose he'd used to wet the smoldering ashes of this morning's gruesome funeral pyre.

Chapter 26

Zoe came downstairs about noon and noticed that Garth was still outside, and the men were still working below. *Guess there's no lunch break for them today,* Zoe thought. *They probably want to get done as quickly as possible.*

Opening the French doors, she called for Garth. He was grateful to hear her voice. He welcomed any reason to distract him from the disgusting job at hand. He was dealing witht he remains of his scorch and burn mission. "I wouldn't come out here quite yet," he warned Zoe when he saw her standing at the door. "I'll come to you."

"I had no intention of coming out there. I just wanted to check on you," she murmured, then hugged him tightly. "I also wanted to tell you that I'm meeting Maggie today for a late lunch."

"Good. Get out of this house. You've had enough surprises for today. They should be finished with the cooler by the time you get back, and I'll have the patio area cleaned up soon, too."

"Garth, you do know this won't end it, right?"

"What won't end?"

"This house is infused with something evil. It's hanging in the air all around us. You feel it, I know you do."

"Look, I don't believe in ghosts, the boogeyman, or the tooth fairy. Everything will be fine. The boys will finished with the cooler, I'll get rid of the mess out here, and we'll all live happily ever after."

"Uh-huh. Oh, I know we'll eventually live happily ever after, but not until we get rid of the evil. I know it's not finished with us yet."

Garth's cell rang, interrupting Zoe's gloom and doom speech. "Hey, Josh. What's up?"

"I got a call from the locals about your 'historic discovery,'" Josh said. *"The county is officially done with everything, and they're turning it over to you. You got a few minutes? I'm meeting Maggie at about four and can stop by before that to deliver your treasure."*

"Sure, I'll be here. I'll tell you all about my new job as a snake wrangler when you get here."

A few minutes later, Zoe said good-bye to Garth and told him she'd be back between 5 and 6 p.m. with takeout.

As her Jeep pulled onto the main road to the village, Josh passed her on his way to her house. The box containing an evil that no one could foresee or understand was riding on the seat next to him.

Garth came from the side of the house to greet Josh as he exited his car. The two men exchanged pleasantries, and then Garth told Josh about the morning's adventures as they walked through the front door.

"What the hell are snakes doing out in mid-November? Aren't they supposed to be hibernating this time of year?"

"I'm no expert, but that sounds right. The whole thing's got Zoe convinced the house is possessed." He emphasized his statement by throwing up his hands with a resounding "Boogity-boogity!"

Josh chuckled, and turned his attention to the large banker's box he was carrying. "It seems, my friend, you are the proud owner of a piece of Long Island history." With that Josh produced a list of bagged and tagged belongings recovered from the Avery's skeletal guest.

Among the rotted and moldy pieces of red fabric were what was left of a wallet with the faint initials "CB," loose buttons, buckles, disintegrating leather gloves, one boot, a gold watch of superior quality, a knife, and six gold sovereigns. "I left what remains of the owner of these treasures back at the station until you decide what to do with him. I doubted Zoe would want Mr. CB in her living room."

"Yeah, that's all I need, something else to spook her."

"Your unwanted guest and his treasure falls within your ownership rights. You may well have something valuable here."

"Well, we'll worry about that later. Right now, let's go check out the cellar and see how the guys are doing with the cooler. They should be just about done."

With that they descended the stairs, as Garth anticipated the end of this nightmare project. They left the box of "treasure" wide open and the stench of rot emanating from it hung in the air.

Chapter 27

Zoe was thrilled to see Maggie so happy. Having her here and the excitement about her engagement had helped her feel a little more whole. After the loss of her father last year, Maggie was just about the only family Zoe had left. Her cousin had become the sister she never had.

Zoe spotted Maggie sitting near the window where the waning November sun spread its inviting warmth. She quickly took her seat opposite her cousin and motioned for the waitress. Maggie had already had ordered a light Chablis and Zoe was in the mood for something more substantial.

"I'll have VSOP on the rocks."

Maggie looked up in surprise. "Holy cow, Zoe, you must be having a bad day."

"You don't know the half of it."

They both ordered chicken salad, and Zoe began the tale of "infestations, nightmares and sick-

119

ness" she and Garth had been experiencing since they moved into their house. "There's something definitely off in that house — it's sinister. It's like there's a veil of evil covering it. I feel like something or someone is watching me all the time. It's almost like I can hear them breathing. Garth thinks I'm crazy."

By this time Maggie was looking at her a bit fish-eyed, as she was on her third drink. "You do know how nutty this all sounds, right? There are no such things as goblins and ghosties," Maggie slurred, and then laughed.

Zoe realized she wasn't going to find an ally for her theory. She did realize how crazy it sounded, and she tried to convince herself it was all just the stress of moving. She thought talking to someone about it would make it go away, but it didn't.

Maggie reached for her ringing cell and found Josh on the other end, reminding her about their appointment. "I've just left Garth's and I'm on my way to the Realtor's office," he told her

"Couldn't ask for better timing. Zoe and I have just finished."

"I'll meet you there in twenty minutes."

When Maggie ended the call, she asked Zoe if she was okay to drive home.

"I am, but I'm going to have a cup of coffee before I leave."

Maggie reached over, gave her cousin a quick kiss and assured her everything was going to be okay. "It's just the stress of the move, honey. Oh, I almost forgot, Josh said they're finished with the wine cellar! He says it looks great. I can't wait to see it. I gotta go or I'm going to be late. By, honey."

Zoe, now completely relaxed, almost had herself convinced things really were okay and she was just being silly. She motioned for the waitress and ordered black coffee. She would spend the next twenty minutes delaying her return home.

Chapter 28

The noxious stench of gasoline, burned snake flesh and scorched earth still hung in the air as Zoe exited her Jeep. It turned her stomach. Her beautiful landscaped yard had been reduced to a serpent funeral pyre.

She turned as she heard the sound of men's voices. Tom and his crew were packing up, so she met them at their truck. She thanked Tom for getting everything finished quickly.

"You're good to go," he said. "I hope you enjoy it." His words were hollow, and he quickly said his goodbyes and headed down the driveway.

Zoe didn't feel like she could enjoy much of anything at the moment. She heard Garth call out to her and hurried through the huge renovated oak door.

He kissed and hugged her, hoping the completion of this final phase of the renovation would see him. Curiosity about the beast faded, as he noticed the twilight sky had turned to night and he realized how hungry he was.

Zoe had forgotten to bring home takeout and he hadn't eaten all day. "Come on," he said as he pulled Zoe up off the couch and jockeyed her to the front door. "Lets' go down to the burger joint on the corner and feed me. We'll be home in an hour, and then we can celebrate being finished with the renovation."

The burger joint was a theme-prompted drive-thru, landscaped to hide all manner of signage and commercialism. Hedges and décor of the building had been modified to meet the historic district's codes. Garth woofed down two Big Macs, fries and a shake before he leaned back in the Jeep with complete satisfaction. The impromptu run for burgers seemed to put them both in a better mood.

Zoe was busy slurping her way through her turtle shake, when laughter seemed to find its way back into their conversation. "Let's go home," Zoe said giggling, as a sly wink and grin punctuated her meaning. She felt like a kid again.

Hugo didn't greet them at the door in his usual fashion, instead he had moved from in front of the an end to her melancholy feelings. He took her directly downstairs and pointed out the cooler with a flourish of his hand and a smile on his face.

As much as Zoe didn't feel like celebrating, she couldn't let her feelings show. She didn't want to ruin the excitement of the moment for Garth. She was happy it was finished, and she mustered enough gusto to show him she meant it. Still, a lingering pall dampened her enthusiasm. "It's wonderful, Garth! Maybe now we can start calling this place home and have a Christmas house-warming party."

Ah, she's back, he thought. "Sounds like a plan. Lets' go upstairs, turn the fire up and check the news."

As they reached the top of the stairs, Hugo stood at the French doors asking to come in. Zoe opened the door and hugged the big dog, talking to him in a lovey-dovey, condescending way. The dog accepted the loving praise, then made his way to his spot in front of the fireplace.

"Well, looks like he's decided to grace us with his presence tonight. Wonder if his buddy is still out there." Garth took a quick peek out the window to see if there was any sign of the wolf, but didn't see fireplace to stand in front of the French doors. Outside, the crescent moon beamed brightly, its light falling on Hugo and the open banker's box in front of him. "What's that?" Zoe inquired as she noticed the box.

Garth explained the treasures Josh had dropped off. "He says there may be something valuable in there."

With her eyes fixed on the box, she approached cautiously, trying to peek inside without touching it. She quickly turned away when she caught a whiff of something nasty. "Ugh, it stinks! You should've left it outside."

"There are a few gold coins in there, so I thought it was better off inside. Of course, the owner of those particular items is still at the station until we can figure out what to do with him."

The thought of the remains found in their cellar made her shudder. There was nothing funny about this whole escapade.

"I thought we could bring him home and give him a name," Garth teased.

"Ha-ha. I just wish we could forget about the whole thing."

"Come on, we can deal with that stuff tomorrow. It's been a long day. I don't want to think about bogeymen, snakes, or bugs any more tonight."

Hand in hand, they climbed the stairs. Usually Hugo wasn't far behind, but not tonight. Tonight he lay with his hair bristling, emitting a low growl.

The wolf was not far away, and he soon approached the patio doors and lay down outside. His presence was calming for Hugo. Like humans, dogs know fear, and tonight Hugo needed reassurance. The two animals were of one mind, and they worked to hold fear and the unknown at bay.

Chapter 29

After a warm shower, the two quickly fell asleep. The events of the day had exhausted them both, and all remnants of romance had been forgotten.

This last month had left them tense and on edge. Uneasy nights and paranoid thoughts constantly plagued Zoe, and Garth couldn't focus at work. Ms. Potter had even noticed he was strangely inattentive to detail at work, and more than once his foreman, Norm, found him preoccupied.

Norm had even been forced to raise his voice to rouse Garth out of a dreamlike state on more than one occasion. Norm had also found building plans with far too many changes — changes that were not only costly, but downright dangerous — as well as material choices that didn't make sense. "What the hell's the matter with him?" he'd complained to Ms. Potter.

"He's just not himself. These drawings are all wrong, and I can't seem to get his attention," she lamented.

They both knew the boss hadn't been himself for at least three weeks. Concern for his health prompted Ms. Potter to call Zoe one morning. Garth Avery was the closest thing to a son Ms. Potter had, and Norm had been his "uncle" from the time Zoe's father brought him on board, and they were both worried.

Zoe, too, had been acting more than a little strange. So much so that friends thought it was more than just stress. They were worried she was heading toward a nervous breakdown, but no one would say it out loud. Concern for her continued to grow, as she became more detached and adamant about something evil inhabiting her home.

Things were going to have to change soon for both of them, and Zoe and Garth both know it. Events seemed to be building toward an ominous conclusion.

The soft glow from a nightlight fought hard to illuminate the encroaching darkness as Zoe and Garth both dreamed of horrible things. Zoe fought through bottomless pits, roamed through tombstones, saw worms and dead cats, and Edgar Alan Poe's stories came back to haunt her. Interspersed with these were visions of the murderous Beckman's skeleton sitting up and croaking, "Dead no more! Dead no more!"

Suddenly, she sat bolt upright, gasping for air. Hugging herself tightly, she tried to calm down, muttering, "It was just a dream." Quietly, so she didn't disturb Garth, she rolled from the bed and went to the bathroom. She moistened a washcloth and blotted her face. It helped, and reality slowly replaced the veil of the surreal, but she knew further sleep would be impossible.

She noticed that Garth seemed to be dreaming, too, as he thrashed around in his sleep. Resigning herself to being awake the rest of the night, she quietly crept down the dimly lit hall to the top of the stairs. When she looked down, she saw Hugo standing there, hackles raised and growling.

She walked down a few steps and saw a filmy mist hovering above the creepy treasure box. As she watched, it grew in depth and intensity. It hung in the air like the Cheshire cat in the movie *Alice in Wonderland.*

When Hugo moved closer to it, a hissing noise came from the mist. Ambient light illuminated the scene, and she saw the black ooze from the wall reaching out to meet the mist in an unholy alliance.

As if a hand from above had taken hold of her, Zoe ran to grab her mother's Bible. Book in hand, she moved with purpose, running down the stairs to stand by Hugo's side.

When she got there, she could see the wolf standing outside the French doors, looking in. She moved to the door, opened it and the wolf charged in. He was immediately on the defensive — teeth flashing and blue eyes blazing.

The mist backed off, seeming to draw back at the wolf's presence, and Zoe quickly turned on all the lights. Like a genie returning to its bottle, the mist spiraled and disappeared. Zoe now knew the evil was real, not just something she'd imagined, and it had taken up residence in her house.

Knowing she wasn't losing her mind made her feel calmer, even though the thought of the evil entity filled her with dread. She knew this was her battle to win, and she wasn't about to give up.

She decided not telling Garth about this latest incident would be prudent. He already doubted her sanity. *Once I figure this out and decide how to get rid of it, I'll tell him,* she thought with resolve. *He wouldn't believe it if I told him now.*

She put a pot of coffee on, found the bleach and set about scrubbing away the offensive black ooze. She worked at it until it was gone. When that was done, she poured a cup of coffee and sat down to read her mother's Bible — something she hadn't done in a long, long time.

Both animals quietly lay at her feet, keeping vigil.

Chapter 30

Garth saw an incredible sight from the top of the stairs. The early morning sun cheerfully splintered through the leaded glass windows, spilling over Zoe and her two protectors. "You're up early," he said. Zoe missed the clarity of the statement through a wide-open yawn. "Who's your new friend?"

Zoe ignored the question as she made her way to the coffee pot to fill his mug. "You look awful."

"Didn't sleep a wink," he muttered.

"Oh, you slept," she said. "You just didn't sleep well. You tossed and turned and mumbled all night."

"Bad dreams."

"Apparently. I had some, too."

"Yeah, Mrs. Potter and Norm were shouting warnings at me, bridges were falling, there were buildings collapsing, sink holes, flooding, machinery stalling, fires, people screaming and running me over in a nightmarish stampede. It was awful."

"Yeah, that sounds bad."

They sat in companionable silence on the couch as they drank their coffee. After a while, Garth said, "I've got to get work." He roused himself from the couch to refill his mug. "There are a lot of things at that need re-evaluating. I've let things slide a bit this month."

Taking his coffee with him, Garth climbed the stairs to go shower and shave. When he came back down, Zoe had a to-go cup ready for him. With a quick kiss, and a curious sideways glance at the wolf that was sleeping on the floor, he left. "See you tonight."

Good, she'd wanted him gone early so he wouldn't be there for what she was about to do. The wolf looked at her and walked to the French doors, asking to go out. Zoe obliged, and when she opened the door, Hugo followed him outside.

The morning light was comforting. *Evil does not fare well in the light of day*, she mused. She knew Garth would think she'd really gone crazy if he saw what she planned to do. Her home was her retreat, a sanctuary, and it was meant to be filled with love and peace. She was not about to have it sullied by otherworldly demon mists. She planned to put the entity on notice.

Like a mad woman, she opened all the windows and doors to let the purifying sun and cold air flow through. A story her mother told her when she was a child had inspired her. Her mother had spoken of a friend who had chased all demons and evil from her home.

She said the lady "called out the devil and all his disciples" who were in her home. Raising the bible high, she commanded, "Be gone! The Lord lives here! Out! Out! Out!"

Her mother told her a great wind blew through the home and all the windows and doors slammed shut. Once that happened, a calm descended. This made her mother a believer, and the story had come to mind just when Zoe needed it.

Though she didn't consider herself fanatically religious, her mother had always told her, "Never underestimate the power of the Lord." With this in mind, Zoe walked to the offending box in the corner where Hugo and the wolf had stood sentry, picked it up and carried it out through the French doors. She opened it in the bright, warm sunshine and looked at the tattered and smelly contents. She then closed it tight and retrieved a roll of duct tape. She taped the box shut and then taped her crucifix to the lid. Once that was done, she went back in the house and left the offending box outside.

Standing in the middle of the room, happy that no one was around to see her performance, she raised her mother's Bible above her head. Spinning to face each corner of the home, she boldly announced, "The Lord God almighty dwells in this house! All vestiges of demons and evil be gone! Be Gone!" She said it three times just to be sure.

Nothing quite as dramatic as a great wind and doors and windows slamming happened, but she felt her ritual couldn't hurt. She wanted to cleanse her home and put the resident evil on notice.

She closed the windows and doors, let Hugo in, and then called Carol at the village museum. She wanted to pay her a visit before her appointment with Father Fitzhugh later that afternoon.

With Thanksgiving at Rachel's coming up the next day, Zoe wanted some peace of mind. She was afraid her home couldn't survive the onslaught of evil if she didn't find a way to remove it soon.

Chapter 31

Zoe met Carol Pangborn at 9:30 and told her about the box of historic treasures. She also mentioned that the remains were still with the police. Carol seemed excited about the coins and buttons — anything pertaining to the Revolutionary War always caught her interest.

Zoe remembered the letter from Prudence and hoped Carol had something else that might tie in with the initials CB, since they were on the leather wallet and the knife. "I think we've found the British Col. Cecil Bradford, or what's left of him," she told Carol.

Carol assured her she would check to see if there was anything at the museum that pertained to the initials CB, and said she would also do an internet search on the name. "You'd be surprised what you can find online. Lots of handwritten things have been digitized, which makes it much easier to search. I'll also contact the British Historical Society and see if they have anything to add.

Zoe thanked her for her help. She just kept thinking about how the 200-year-old letter penned by a young girl named Prudence so closely described what she was going through. As the girl had put it, "There is a maelstrom of evil surrounding us."

She left Mrs. Pangborn happily engrossed in her research. Zoe knew it was something she loved doing and got the impression the woman lived for it.

When she left the museum's parking lot, Zoe wheeled the Jeep around and headed for the city. She didn't want to keep Father Fitzhugh waiting.

When she entered the sanctity of the church and holy surroundings, she was reminded of how inconsequential and petty we all are. *The whole world is always reaching out and begging for salvation and answers to their prayers, but none of them will work to save themselves,* she mused.

Father Fitzhugh greeted her with his great booming voice, hugged her and, of course, scolded her as he always did for not visiting sooner. They talked for a long time, recalling her childhood and parents.

He knew she was having difficulty bringing up whatever what was on her mind, so he finally dropped all pretense of reminiscing and gently coaxed it from her.

"Father," she began, "please don't think I'm crazy, but I believe our home is possessed by a demon. I can feel an evil growing in our home, and it's getting stronger every day."

Father Fitzhugh looked at her intently, his eyes urging her to go on. The damn burst, and teary-eyed, she confided all the horrible things that had happened, including uncovering the skeleton, the nightmares, sleepless nights and sickness. "We've also had a plague of snakes and bugs of biblical proportions. Plus, there have been electrical and plumbing failures from the time we moved in, Father."

She even mentioned the ever-present wolf. Finally, she told him about the box of historic items they'd found with the skeleton and the way the mist had seemed to come from it the previous night.

"Father, there's also a black oozing substance coming out of the wall and we can't get rid of. It comes back again and again, regardless of how we clean it. Last night, that weird mist seemed to be drawn it, as well as the box. I think everything in the box belonged to the same man who had the initials CB.

"I haven't told Garth this, but I took the box and its contents outside, taped it shut and then taped my crucifix to the top. I left it there, in direct sunlight."

Father Mike nodded his head approvingly. Unbeknownst to Zoe, he felt she had bought some time by doing that.

"Do you believe me, Father?" she asked imploringly.

He took her by the hand to quiet her and she said, "I need you, Father. Come to our home and bless it. We need you to help us get rid of whatever is plaguing us."

The intensity of her confession, and release of her burden to Father Fitzhugh took a weight off her shoulders. *He didn't treat my confession with cynicism. I now clearly have an ally in this fight!* Relief flooded her.

The Father walked her to the door and assured her everything would be all right, but didn't go into detail as to how this would come about. "You should enjoy your Thanksgiving holiday with your friends and family. I'll contact you next week to make arrangements for the blessing."

"Father, you should come and have Thanksgiving with us. We're all going to Rachel's house. We'd love to have you join us."

"I'll think about it and let you know," he said as he walked her out.

Zoe left the rectory, relieved and content in the knowledge that Father Fitzhugh's visit would remove the evil from their lives.

Now, she felt free to concentrate on enjoying Thanksgiving She mentally made a short list of things she could bring for the Thanksgiving meal and happily went on her way. She'd decided to get a little gift for Carol Pangborn and drop it off before she headed home.

Father Fitzhugh, on the other hand, fretted and clutched his rosary. He would not rest easy tonight. He believed every word Zoe said. He knew the dangers he was facing in that house. This was no small task Zoe had set for him. There were definitely powerful forces of evil at work.

The Prince of Darkness had tested the strength of the Lord many times over the millennia. Father Fitzhugh knew he'd been chosen as the Lord's defender and messenger in this fight, so he prayed for strength.

Chapter 32

Z oe opened the door to Carol's world, carrying the beautiful flower arrangement she'd bought to thank her for her efforts. She quietly called Carol's name, and found her in a dusty back corner of the building. She was smiling broadly, wearing an unmistakable look of satisfaction.

"The archives gave up three more letters," Carol told Zoe. "They refer to a Col. Cecil Bradford. All three letters mention him in some way and all say he was extremely brutal when dealing with both soldiers and members of the colony.

"Hangings, torture, separating fathers from children and wives, and leaving the settlements with no food or livestock are only a few of his bloody escapades," she continued excitedly. "One letter, from a British infantryman, spoke in detail about Bradford and his harsh and inhumane treatment of his troops."

She told Zoe she'd emailed her friend who was an expert on British military history and asked about anyone with the initials C.B. with the rank of Colonel during the war. "I asked her to look especially at those who were listed as missing, dead, or unaccounted for. It may be a couple of days, but she'll definitely get back with me."

"That's great," Zoe said. "I wanted to give you these," she continued, holding out the bouquet, "to thank you for all the research you've been doing for me."

"Oh, these are beautiful! They can be my Thanksgiving centerpiece tomorrow. Would you like copies of these letters?"

"Yes. Thank you so much, Carol."

Mrs. Pangborn looked at the time and gasped. "I have to get going, it's getting late. My kids and grandkids will be at the house tomorrow and I've got a lot to do before then."

They left the museum together, and Carol thanked Zoe again for the flower arrangement.

Zoe headed home, since it was nearly 5 p.m. and she expected Garth to be home early. Her visit with Father Mike had given her some solace. Tonight, hopefully she and Garth would find a peaceful sleep.

When she pulled into the driveway, the feeling of dread didn't greet her. Only the faint odor of gasoline remained hanging in the air as a gruesome reminder of the invading reptiles.

An almost full moon was already visible in the sky, and the light was nearly gone. The new exterior lights Garth had installed came to life as she got out of her vehicle, and she sighed in relief. She hadn't wanted to walk in the near darkness.

For the first time in weeks, Zoe felt happy — really happy — when she entered her home. As she turned to close the door, she glanced out at the night sky and saw a lone snowflake fall lazily through the darkness — the first of the season. A smile came slowly to her lips. *A fire would feel good tonight.*

Chapter 33

The night passed without incident, and Zoe and Garth enjoyed the evening. They caught up on the news, and Garth recounted his day. He'd accomplished a lot, and had also caught a lot of mistakes he'd made in the last month.

"I'm completely to blame," he said. "My mind had to be on another planet. Norm and Mrs. Potter both tried to talk to me about it, and for some reason I just wouldn't listen."

"I know the feeling, we've neither one been ourselves lately. By the way, I love the exterior lights. This old place is really starting to feel like home. I'm look forward to our holidays here."

"I feel pretty good tonight, too," Garth said. "I wished Norm, Mrs. Potter *and* Klaus a happy Thanksgiving and sent them your love."

"You mean Klaus from last year? Our Klaus, the 'chocolate vendor' Klaus?"

Garth nodded his head with a big grin on his face. "They're going to Germany for the holidays. It wouldn't surprise me if they came back married. Uncle Norm is going to descend on his brother and their brood, so I closed the doors for the next week. We got all the loose ends and paperwork dealt with today and I thought we could all use a break."

"It feels good to feel good, doesn't it?"

"Yep. I'm looking forward to taking Josh on at poker tomorrow, while you girls do 'women things' in the kitchen."

"Chauvinist!" They were having a good evening. Something they hadn't had in a long time.

"We might even go buy a tree this weekend."

Zoe squealed at the idea of their first Christmas in their new home. "A *big* one," she chimed in.

Switching topics, Zoe said, "Rachel expects us about one tomorrow. She said not to worry about bringing anything, but I did get some fresh flowers, wine and cheese. I got enough for us tonight, too," she added as she set out crackers, olives, and cheese. "We'll eat light tonight, so we can enjoy the fruits of Rachel's labors tomorrow."

While they ate, Zoe briefly filled Garth in about her visit with Father Fitzhugh, and told him she had invited him to bless their house.

"It certainly could use a blessing after all the aggravation it's given us," Garth commented. "I always look forward to seeing him and hearing his outlandish Irish tales."

Later, Hugo was waiting at the door for his final call of nature for the night. As Garth opened it for him, the wolf came to greet him. While Hugo hurried off into the woods, the wolf softly padded up to the door and sat at attention at Garth's feet. Garth still couldn't comprehend the familiarity they were experiencing with this wild animal.

Slowly, he extended his hand to touch the wolf, and immediately felt the strangest feeling of peace wash over him. The animal radiated a warmth and security Garth couldn't explain. When Hugo returned, Garth opened the door wide for both animals.

They lay together, alert, as Zoe and Garth climbed the stairs for the evening.

Across the way, Father Fitzhugh fretted. He couldn't sleep until the task of cleansing the evil from Zoe's home was resolved. "God protect Your two children, Garth and Zoe," he whispered quietly into the night. He remembered telling Zoe to keep her Bible close as he'd pressed his rosary into her hand. *The beast will not be kept at bay for long,* the Father thought. *Satan never sleeps.*

Chapter 34

Zoe and Garth both slept soundly again, and on Thanksgiving morning they awoke refreshed and hungry. Both were denying themselves, in anticipation of Rachel's glorious bird.

There was a light dusting of snow outside, and Zoe was genuinely happy this morning as she opened the French doors for both animals. The crisp air caught her by surprise, and she quickly closed the door, catching a glimpse of the box she'd left outside as she did. Oddly, it seemed to have moved, and it wasn't covered with snow.

Her phone rang, and Father Mike greeted her in his bold Irish brogue, "Good mornin', darlin'. I'm sorry to call so early, but the conversation we had yesterday got me to thinking and praying. I don't want to alarm you, but I think you need to keep your bible and my rosary close to you today. Check the security of the box, too, and if need be, tape it again. Cover it, too, and place another cross on it, if you have one.

"But, Father Mike—"

"Please, girl, just do it for me. You enjoy yourself today. I won't be able to make it. I'll contact you tomorrow."

She said goodbye to Father Mike just as Garth came down the stairs. "Who would call this early on Thanksgiving morning?"

"That was Father Fitzhugh. He was just wishing us happy Thanksgiving. He appreciated our invitation to dinner, but won't be able to make it."

"Well, he'll be missing one fine meal." Garth stretched broadly, and yawned. "Last night was the best sleep I've had in what seems like a month!"

There was a smile on his face, which Zoe hadn't seen for some time. They were both happy this fine Thanksgiving morning.

Garth reached for her and hugged her tightly. "I'm hungry as a bear. Can I at least have some toast?" he pleaded.

"Oh, okay. But that's it — just enough to take the edge off. Why don't you check the time for the parade?"

Before he left the room, Zoe said, "I forgot to tell you, I checked with Carol Pangborn regarding the skeleton and treasure bits we found, and she's doing some research. She found some old letters in the archives, and we think he may have been a British Colonel by the name of Cecil Bradford. She also put a call in to someone at the British Historical Society. We may hear something from them by the first of the week.

"Oh, I put that smelly old box outside so it didn't stink things up in here."

"Well good, it just suits me fine to get that stuff out of here, it's caused us enough problems," Garth said as he wolfed down his toast.

"It seems this Colonel, if it is him, was a horrible, wicked man who brought death and starvation to the early settlers in this area. He hung the men folk, raided their supplies, and left many of the townspeople to die."

"Sounds like a lovable sort," Garth muttered to himself. "Hope the museum takes him and his things."

"I'll talk to her about that the first of the week."

"Hey, I'm going to go get cleaned up. Just casual, right?"

"Right," Zoe said as she peeked out the French doors. She would do what Father Mike told her to do while Garth was in the shower.

She retrieved the roll of duct tape and re-taped the box several times on all sides. She then went to get the crucifix from her childhood out of her jewelry box. She taped it securely to the box, too, before covering it with a tarp. She didn't question the Father's instructions.

When her task was complete, Hugo was at her side ready to go inside. His companion, the wolf, remained at the perimeter of the patio. She put her bible in her purse so she wouldn't forget it when they left for Rachel's.

She set the flowers, wine, beer and assorted goodies together on the counter, and hurried to get dressed.

She couldn't believe how gaining Father Mike's help had eased her mind, and made her outlook positive. Thanksgiving with family and loved ones was just the tonic she needed.

Chapter 35

Father Mike had heard about unusual happenings, viral outbreaks, sickness, grisly deaths, unexplained mental disorders and all sorts of things that couldn't easily be discounted as coincidence from other priests. There was always priestly gossip that said these sightings, actions, and mysterious behaviors, had been witnessed by the highest in the church hierarchy. He also knew the Devil likes to make mischief, and thought that was what was going on at Zoe's house.

The ancient enemy's antics spread quickly these days, aided by the speed of email and hi-tech contact, he thought. *But, this instance is far older and more insidious than anything on the internet.*

Zoe's cryptic and frightening descriptions of the strange happenings at her home, the unearthing of a tomb and the veritable plagues of insects and vermin had all the markings of the devil at play. He worried that merely blessing the house might not be enough to exorcise the demon. Demonic presences were not to be taken lightly.

He knew that Zoe was far too level headed to come to him in such a state were she not convinced this was truly an evil entity. Zoe was like his daughter, and he'd seen her through the death of her parents and many other aspects of her life, so he was confident he was reading the situation correctly.

I must consult the Bishop, he thought. *Any interaction or dialogue with an emissary of Satan, fallen angels or demons, can indeed be dangerous. I'm going to consult the church archives and study all procedures. I also might need the youth and strength of another priest to be victorious.*

Chapter 36

Thanksgiving had a Norman Rockwell-like feel to it. The boys all came to greet them at the door, and Maggie and Josh were in the kitchen helping Rachel.

When Garth and Zoe appeared, Josh yelled out to them as if they were jailers come to give him freedom. "Glad you're here! Now, maybe we'll be released from this prison known as the kitchen. Zoe, can you throw me a lifeline?"

Setting everything on the counter, Zoe dutifully moved in, removing the knife from Josh's "unskilled" hands. "Thank you, I'm much better at preparing briefs," he joked.

The boys each grabbed a beer, and retreated to the other room as the girls shooed them out. Rachel was checking her "masterpiece," a 25-pounder. It was beautifully browned, and Zoe and Maggie marveled at her skills. "She makes it look so easy," Zoe said.

This was not idle praise. Rachel was a sorceress at cooking and presenting beautiful meals. Maggie and Zoe just looked on. "Last time I tried to cook a turkey, it was not a pretty sight," Maggie said.

"How's the house hunting coming?" Zoe casually asked Maggie.

"I think we've got it narrowed down to two. Could you come with me on Saturday and take a look?"

"I'd love to. We'll make a day of it."

Both got back to the business at hand, and with Rachel's direction, managed to get all the side dishes onto the table along with the beautiful bird.

Josh and Rachel sat at the head of the table, with Peter, Nicky and Lech on one side and Maggie, Zoe and Garth facing them. They all seemed happy this year. After the terrible incidents and issues of the previous year, all of them were grateful for the positive changes in their lives.

The three boys Rachel had taken in were getting past their former abuse and starvation, and were healthy and secure. Beckman's abuse was all but forgotten, and their nightmares had finally been replaced by pleasant sleep. Lech, the twin's older brother, had even found peace with his murderous action toward Beckman, who was a killer and child molester.

These children had given Rachel a new lease on life. She had worked with them so that they now spoke almost flawless English and were earning good grades in school. They had accepted Rachel as their parent and guardian, and returned the love they received from her eagerly. They looked to Josh as their older brother, and Maggie was quickly making inroads toward their acceptance, too.

Josh and Maggie were looking forward to their wedding, and Garth and Zoe were finally feeling like their life in their new home was coming together.

They all had much to be grateful for.

Josh did the honors and said grace. They bowed their heads and all of them thought about the good things in their lives before they dug in.

Between all "the pass the potatoes and pass the gravy," conversation seemed to revolve mostly around the upcoming wedding. Zoe did little to contribute to the conversation about their new home, other than to say she'd invited Father Fitzhugh to bless it. When anyone tried to bring up their recent issues, she quickly changed the subject.

Josh asked about the box, and Zoe told him about Carol Pangborn's efforts. "She said she might have a little more information for us next week. We're happy to give everything to the museum." After that, the topic was dropped. Zoe didn't want to spoil the day with more talk about that hateful box.

When they'd finished eating, they gave Rachel her just rewards in praise. Rachel "took her bow" graciously. The men escorted her to the living room and gave her strict orders not to worry about cleanup. "You won't get an argument from me. Just be careful with the good china and glassware."

After cleanup, the men retreated to play poker, and Lech sat in to learn the basics. Both Garth and Josh knew he would rather be playing on his computer. Nicky and Peter found things to do outside, and Maggie, Zoe and Rachel huddled in front of the TV, watching an old Turner Classic movie. Later, Maggie and Zoe bundled up like the kids and took a short walk.

When everyone had room in their stomachs for more food, Rachel called them all in for coffee and desert.

Chapter 37

Later that evening, they turned into their well-lit driveway and then walked up to their softly illuminated entry. Zoe and Garth opened the large oak front door, arms laden with leftover Thanksgiving goodies. They'd been given enough food to fill their refrigerator. It was far too much to contemplate after their large dinner. Garth deposited the basket on the counter for examination and snacks later.

Zoe opened French doors wide and let Hugo out. The night air hung crisp and clear around her, and a huge alabaster moon washed its light over the landscape. Zoe could clearly see the wolf standing at the bottom of the patio stairs. Hugo went to greet him, and the two seemed to be engrossed in highly sophisticated canine conversation.

She shivered and closed the door, then turned to Garth to complain about how much she'd eaten.

Both retreated to the couch in front of the large fireplace. Garth pressed the remote, and an inviting fire sprang to life.

Zoe put on her favorite "elevator music" that was peppered with Sinatra, Martin, Bublé, Stewart and some easy jazz favorites. "Looks like our friend and Hugo will be out there for a while."

"That's fine with me. We can just kick back, relax and have some alone time," Garth said, lazily kicking off his shoes. "I can't tell you what a good — no *great* — day I've had. It seems like since we moved in this place I haven't had a peaceful moment, here or at work."

"I know, I know. Staying here with the construction going on day after day, along with all the weird stuff that's been happening has grated on my last nerve. That terrible thing in the cellar we unearthed, plus the bugs, being ill, and all the aggravation — it was almost too much. I tell you, Garth, there's an evil presence here."

"Now, don't start that again. The only boogeyman around here is me," he said, grabbing her playfully. He pulled her down to him, awash in her giggles. "Boo!" he shouted. She laughed and nestled in his arms, the place she felt most secure in the world.

All fear and regrets about the house and all its inherent weirdness disappeared when Garth kissed her. Nothing bad could or would harm her when Garth was here.

Making love had been nonexistent since they moved into this house. Now, it felt so normal and so right. Afterward, the fire burned bright and sleep embraced them.

Zoe stirred from sleep and noticed the clock. It was almost midnight, and she and Garth had never made it to bed. Opening the French doors, she called for Hugo. He was immediately at the door with the wolf at his side. He came in, but the wolf remained outside. The invitation to come in was open to him, but he turned and melted into the darkness.

"Your friend wants to take guard duty tonight," she whispered to Hugo. "I think we should all go to bed."

Garth woke up when Hugo gave him a wet kiss. He got up and they climbed the stairs together, with Hugo on their heels. "Since you've had such a good day, maybe you might want to pick out our first Christmas tree tomorrow," Zoe said. She was trying to get as much mileage out of his good mood as possible. This was their first Thanksgiving as a married couple, and the first in their new home. It was a time she wanted to remember with warm feelings, but the feeling of foreboding was slowly returning. *Garth may think he's the only boogeyman here, but I know better.*

When they'd gone upstairs and turned off the lights, the black ooze reappeared downstairs. Outside, the covered box remained subdued, but the wolf wasn't fooled and he kept watch.

Chapter 38

Prudence Farthington was a young and truly beautiful fifteen year old. Her hair was pale blonde and her eyes were the color of the cornflowers that grew abundantly in the fields of the township. She, like so many of the settlers in the colonies, lived off the land. She'd come here with few possessions. Her family wasn't destitute but they certainly didn't come from a position of wealth.

The well-educated family had been lured to the Americas, just as many had been, looking for a less oppressive life than they had in England. Once here, the family attended all the secret meetings and rallies about freedom from the crown's onerous oversight and heavy taxes. The King's men were ever-watchful, and Prudence and her family had several visits from the Redcoats due to suspicion of treason against King George.

Each time, Col. Cecil Bradford headed the inspection and harassed the family. These visits always left the Farthington household in turmoil. Much was confiscated, and the Farthingtons feared for their lives. Instructions from her father directed Prudence, her sister and two brothers to stay close to home and be constantly vigilant. Their father, of course, continued his fight with the Patriots against the Redcoats in secret.

Unfortunately, Prudence did not go unnoticed by the Colonel. The unsolicited break-ins and harassment were not so much due to suspicion of treason, but because of Bradford's lust for Prudence.

While her family trembled before Bradford's wrath, the young woman challenged him with hate in her eyes, vowing revenge should her mother and family be harmed. While her father was gone, she stood between the imposing Colonel and her helpless family. If Prudence could have killed with her eyes, the Colonel knew he would be dead many times over.

When her father returned after the latest harassment, preparations were made for a safe place where the family could hide if the soldiers came again. A small burrow was hollowed out in the woods beyond the fields. This would be the place they would run to if they needed safety.

Things were quiet for the next few weeks, and the war and savagery seemed to move further inland. The township folks had all but relaxed, since news of the war was hard to come by. What they did learn came secondhand from travelers and rumor.

Prudence's father had been gone for a month and the family was holding on with hope and a prayer. The people of their small village had also found hope through prayers for peace and independence, so they began erecting a church.

One quiet Sunday morning during the service in the half completed church, Col. Bradford returned with his men. The pastor and his flock had barely said amen when the thundering hooves of his bri-gade made their presence known. Col. Bradford certainly made no attempt to return to town in a gentlemanly fashion.

Unceremoniously, he ordered his men to dis-mantle and burn the partially built place of worship. The minister and some of his flock looked on, while others ran and sought cover.

Apparently, the Colonel and his men were in retreat, and his orders were to destroy and/or confiscate any and all things of value in the name of the King.

Prudence, her mother and her siblings warily made their way back to their home, while Bradford and his men were busy burning the church and "confiscating" for the crown.

As twilight approached, the town was left in ashes and despair. Col. Bradford, his work finished, took his men and made his way to the Farthington farm.

The Colonel saw the mother and her children at the top of the hill, and it was far too late for them to run for cover. Bradford spurred his horse up the hill, sword drawn and icy blue eyes showing no mercy.

Mother, the two older children, and the toddler fell quickly to his blade. Without dismounting, he pursued a guaranteed kill. A soul-wrenching scream rang through the valley as Prudence scrabbled for footing. Bloodied sword held high, the Colonel urged his lathered horse forward, and the evil visage of Col. Cecil Bradford bore down on Prudence.

When he reached her, he savagely maimed her and then raped her. Other than the screams and slice of the sword, the world went silent. This was evil at its finest, and the devil took note.

Chapter 39

Zoe and Garth awoke to a sunny Friday morning. Both had slept without incident, and were eagerly looking forward to the long weekend. Zoe snuggled close to Garth and with girlish enthusiasm gave him an early wake up call.

The high November sun flooded through the windows, adding fuel to her already cheery mood. The prospect of a long ride in the country with Garth and the choosing of their first Christmas tree for their new home almost erased any worries she had about the house.

She quickly dressed and said, "I'll be downstairs when you're ready. I saw the Boy Scouts had a tree lot in the village," she added before she left the room with Hugo at her feet.

A muffled groan came from Garth's side of the bed.

"I heard that!"

Her head popped around the door. "Oh, come on," she chided. "You promised." She reached over and tweaked him on the nose, and then ran away, leaving him whining and feigning disapproval.

Zoe's sunny mood quickly disappeared as she reached the bottom step and the black ooze came into view. It had made its way to the top of the circular stairwell leading down to the cellar again. Hugo made a deep growl of disapproval, and Zoe understood how he felt.

She opened the French doors for him and he joined the wolf, who was steadfastly alert in his role as guardian. Zoe began to feel afraid. Steeling herself, she thought, *I will* not *be intimidated by this unnatural invasion of my home!*

Quickly, before Garth came down, she scrubbed the disgusting ooze with bleach. It was like an invading army that was pushed back in retreat, only to regroup, gather forces and charge again. The stuff was black, gooey and thick. The smell of it took her breath away and nausea followed.

She struggled to recover as she heard Garth coming down the stairs. She walked over to the French doors, opened them and breathed deeply. The bit-ing cold air took care of the nausea, and she put her cheery demeanor back in place.

"What? No coffee?" he quizzed.

"Haven't put it on yet. I've been waiting for your special touch."

"Why? You want a cappuccino?"

"I'd love one. There's whipped cream in the fridge."

"While you're doing that, I'm going to call Father Mike. I think he's coming on Monday."

"Okay, it will be ready when you come back.

The complete disgust she'd just felt caused an overwhelming need to talk to the priest. When she phoned, the reassuring voice of Father Mike came booming through, immediately calming her.

Knowing he was her ally in this fight, she quickly relayed the latest on the black ooze. The priest listened intently. He was gravely concerned about this latest development, because in Catholic dogma it sounded like it was a wanna-be demon. The ooze in itself was no real danger, but it was worrisome that it sought to partner with evil. Given the right circumstances it would couple with the evil entity and become a true Minion of Darkness.

Father Mike remembered Zoe saying it seemed to be connected with the skeletal remains of the British soldier, too. This was a curious situation, but no more strange than stories he'd heard from priests and bishops around the globe. There were all sorts of reports, and there seemed to be a rise in the number of ghastly deaths, sickness and plague. Drought, floods and starvation had also increased worldwide. *The Prince of Darkness is indeed in a mischievous mood lately.*

"Stay calm, darlin'," he said soothingly. "Do as we discussed. Check the covering and cross on the box and keep it outside your home. Be sure to leave both crucifixes attached to the box, too."

"I'll do that, Father."

"Enjoy your home, friends and family this weekend and I will be there Monday to bless your home."

"That's just what I'll do, Father. I'm going to look at homes with my cousin Maggie tomorrow and we'll probably be talking about her wedding, too."

"Fine, fine. I'll look forward to seeing you on Monday."

Relieved, Zoe returned to Garth and the special concoction he'd made for her. He was seated in front of the fire, reading a book. When she came in, he offered her the steaming cup. It was warm and sweet on her tongue. She nestled down beside him and kissed him warmly. Finding the perfect Christmas tree could wait a little longer.

Before they left, Zoe called Maggie about their date to look at houses on Saturday. Maggie had made it clear to Josh that she wouldn't be happy without a job, so she planned to renew her Realtor's license. She'd already made herself familiar with the rural offerings of upstate New York as she looked for her own home. "I have a couple more to see, Zoe. You can give me your thoughts after we give them a look."

"Great, I look forward to tomorrow. In the meantime, Garth and I are in pursuit of the tallest tree in Suffolk. See you tomorrow."

It was well past eleven when Zoe and Garth bundled up and headed out to track down their tree. The Village was busy, and Zoe noticed the Boy Scout's tree lot was jumping.

They pulled in and parked the SUV as close as they could to the lot. Zoe quickly made her way through the rows of balsam pines, firs and evergreens to what seemed to be the one and only tree of her dreams. Her eyes grew bright as she looked at it.

The tree was noticeably removed from the rest. It had to be 25 feet tall. Without saying a word, she turned to Garth. He only shook his head and groaned. "When do you want it delivered?" he asked.

"Tuesday will be fine. Now, let's get something to eat. I'm hungry."

As they drove through the Village, they passed the small museum, causing Zoe to think about the awful box sitting on her patio.

She tried hard the rest of the afternoon to maintain her sunny mood.

Chapter 40

Garth rose early, ready for a quick run. He and running had a dubious relationship. He liked keeping in shape, but was not fanatical about it. When he felt the need, like after an over-indulgence, he would put on his running shoes, mark a couple of miles and do sit ups, always wishing he were more disciplined. The spirit moved him this morning.

Zoe was still sleeping soundly and he was looking forward to fresh air filling his lungs. He always felt better after a run. Slipping on his favorite old sweatshirt, he motioned to Hugo, who was waiting patiently to go outside.

Downstairs, Garth let the big dog out and he met the ever-present wolf. Garth was becoming used to the big animal's calming presence.

He quickly made and chugged down a cup of coffee and opened the newly refurbished front door with its highly polished lion's head doorknocker. Before he took off, he took the time to appreciate the quality work his contractor had done in rehabbing the old oak door.

In truth, Garth realized he hadn't really given the old house the appreciation it deserved. His contractors had done it proud and brought it back to life. *I guess all the aggravation was worth it*, he thought with a nod of approval. He stepped out onto his slate porch, took a deep breath and started jogging slowly to warm up.

Having a few days off from the business was giving him time to stop and smell the roses, so to speak. He was glad to be home. The fresh air and blood rush took hold as he made his way down the drive, noting the sad looking mailbox. It was a stark reminder that it was the one thing he'd failed to replace. *I can remedy that this weekend*, he thought. *I'll make a stop at the village hardware today.*

Curiosity replaced renovation thoughts as he noticed something at the end of the driveway. What he saw as he drew closer had been a thing of magnificent beauty, but now the huge stag lay lifeless, its deep eyes staring right at him. A doe lay next to it, her eyes wide in fright, and a young fawn that was just losing its spots, lay beside her.

As he got closer, he saw that their throats had been cut, and recoiled in horror. When he recovered, he laid his hand on one of the animals. It was still warm. The stag's antlers showed he was a warrior and survivor. *This kill was recent. Who could've done this? It wasn't for food, that's for sure. What a senseless and cruel waste.*

His run forgotten, Garth returned to the house, where he called the village police station and animal control. When he finished, he thought, *Zoe mustn't see this.*

He met the officer at the end of the driveway so Zoe wouldn't be curious about what was going on. This was the same guy who'd responded when they found the skeleton. He assured Garth the animals would be removed as quickly as possible.

Garth thanked the officer for his help and went back in the house. As he walked through the door, a feeling of dread enveloped him. *Could Zoe be right? This house has brought us nothing but grief. I think maybe there is something here, a wickedness you can't see.*

He turned and saw Hugo at the French doors. He let the big dog in, and the wolf quickly followed, looking directly into Garth's eyes. He seemed to be saying all would be well. The animal's calming essence worked its magic and Garth felt a little better.

He called both animals to the kitchen and gave them some treats. Enjoying their company, he turned his thoughts to Zoe. *I hope she's having sweet dreams.*

Chapter 41

About ten o'clock, Zoe came downstairs. She was fully rested, dressed and feeling sunny. She'd taken a sleep aid and it had allowed her to enjoy a quiet night. She rarely depended upon medication, but since their move to this house she noticed she had started to depend on it more and more. It was the only way she could avoid the nightmares.

She found Garth in his office, reviewing a few prospects for the New Year. "It's about time you got out of bed," he said. "You look like you had a good night."

"Oh, I did. I dreamed of you all night," she said playfully, looking at him doe-eyed and fluttering her eyelashes.

"You did? Well in that case, I should've kept you awake all night."

She dropped in his lap, gave him a quick peck on the cheek. "I can't stay here with you too long. Maggie should be here in an hour. We're going to look at some houses she and Josh are interested in. Can I get you anything from the kitchen before I go?"

"No, I'm fine. As a matter of fact, I'm taking care of a honey-do project today. Thought I'd go in and pick up a mailbox. The original one looks pretty bad."

"That's a great idea," she shot back with her approval. "That rusty old thing does not exactly do justice to this grand old lady."

Garth nodded in agreement. He was glad to see his wife in a good mood and smiling. He tried to dismiss the earlier incident of the butchered deer as just some sick individual's idea of a joke. He didn't think they'd been there long enough to make enemies or anger the neighbors — they hadn't even met all of them yet, but they planned to remedy that soon.

Zoe had plans to incorporate a Christmas get-together with family and friends and extend an open invitation to the surrounding neighbors to drop by for an official meet-and-greet. Recent happenings had reduced her talk of such things, though. *Maybe, just maybe all this nonsense about evil, ghosts and demonic takeovers is done*, Garth thought. *I haven't heard her talk about it lately, which is good. I was starting to worry about her. Maybe the holidays will set things back on an even keel and end the string of bad luck we've had lately. That's all it is, too — it's certainly not the devil, for God's sake.*

A knock of the giant Lion's head announced Maggie's arrival, and Garth quickly opened the door. It had been cold when he went for his run earlier, but it seemed like the temperature had dropped even more when he let Maggie in. "Brrr," she said as she stepped through the door.

"Come on in, Mags. Want some coffee or hot chocolate before we go?" Zoe asked when she greeted Maggie.

As the girls were talking, Maggie looked in amazement through the French doors. "Zoe, is this what you were telling me about?" Hugo and the wolf were posted outside the door, side by side, surveying the field.

"Uh-huh. Isn't he something?"

Garth opened the door and Hugo waltzed in. The wolf sat outside, not willing to abandon his post.

"This is a first. Bet you're the only one around here with a friendly wolf at her door."

Zoe chuckled, "Bet I am, too. He just showed up one day and hasn't left our doorstep. He and Hugo seem to have a talk every morning. It's actually pretty amazing.

"You ready to go? I can't wait to see what you've picked out."

Zoe kissed Garth on her way out and said she'd call later. "Please don't get an ordinary plain mailbox."

Garth knew exactly what this meant. "Don't worry, I'll get something to meet milady's approval." She smiled smugly and headed out the door with Maggie.

Garth hoped the ground wasn't going to be too frozen to dig the hole for the new mailbox post, then followed the girls out the door. As he drove down the driveway, he began making mental notes of his hardware needs until his thoughts were interrupted as he passed the spot where he'd found the butchered deer.

Chapter 42

"Well. It's official," Maggie chirped. "You are now looking at a certified and licensed real estate agent *and* broker, I might add. I got my test results yesterday."

"That's wonderful, Maggie! You've been going at it pretty hard all year."

"I'm really happy. It's one of the best presents I could get for Christmas. I can relax a little now, and start thinking about the wedding. I've been too nervous about passing the test to be excited about it. There's still so much to do before I say 'I Do' and now I'm nervous about it! I love him so much, Zoe."

"I'm happy for both of you, Maggie. Josh is a good man. You couldn't ask for better."

"That's not what you thought in the beginning," Maggie teased. They both laughed. "Josh was telling me about your dinner with him at Rembrandt's after the fundraiser."

"Oh, yes. Back then, I had a very different view of him."

"Thank God those days are over."

"He's become my best friend, Maggie. You know the things he's seen Garth and me through."

"Yes, I know all about the Beckman thing."

"He was a horrible man, Maggie. He was my father's biggest competitor and he was as crooked as they come. Josh was his attorney, you know. Because of that, I wanted nothing but bad luck to come to Mr. Josh Lawton.

"But, in the end, Josh exposed him as the murderer and pervert he was. Beckman's death was a blessing to us all. It released Josh from an untenable promise he made to his father, and saved those three boys. Now they've brought new meaning to his mother's life. I know he's a good man now."

Zoe took a deep breath and continued, "When you came to last year's barbecue, it was a new beginning for Rachel and Josh, and he couldn't have met you at a better time. You two are going to be great together. It didn't hurt that you brought Chloe along that first time you met him, either. You know how he loves animals."

Maggie smiled thinking about Chloe, her Irish setter, and the introduction that changed her life.

"Hey, it just dawned on me that there's only a month left before your wedding. You'd better get busy, woman!"

"I know. What do you think I've been telling you? I'm a nervous wreck!"

"We've got a lot to get accomplished before the end of the year. I just mailed the shower invitations. Rachel and I have it all planned. I know Garth has something up his sleeve for Josh and the boys, too. Riza may show up for the celebration, too. Not many can say they have a Saudi Prince come to their bachelor party."

Maggie was remembering the stories Josh had told her about Garth and the oil field fires in the Middle East. He'd worked on the oil rigs with her Uncle Warren. "You know, Zoe, it's amazing how you all came together and ended up such good friends, especially when things started out with a lot of hate and misunderstandings."

"Yes, it is. Once Beckman was gone, though, everything became clear. He'd been a curse on both families for years. Dad dealt with him and his corruption in the building business, and Josh had to deal with him because he was his law firm's client. Beckman was a degenerate with a cancerous soul. He brought nothing but misery to every person came into contact with."

"Wow!" Maggie had to chuckle at Zoe choice of words. "So, he was a bad guy?"

"How about horrible, terrible, awful, tainted, perverted, deviant, ungodly, satanic— Shall I go on? He abused and maimed children for God's sake. I wish him only hellfire and damnation."

Zoe was thinking about what he'd done to Lech, Peter and Nicky. Josh's guardianship had saved them from a lifetime of despair. "Maggie, you wouldn't believe the condition those children were in when Josh rescued them. Lech, as you know, was responsible for Beckman's death. He'd seen Beckman torture his twin brothers, and he couldn't stand it for one more minute. Beckman paid for their horrible treatment with his life. All of his sins and murders came to light in that old schoolhouse. May he rot in hell."

Zoe shuddered. Thinking about all of that again was almost too much. Taking a deep, cleansing breath, she said, "Now, let's turn our conversation to happier subjects. We haven't picked your cake out yet!"

Maggie, who was usually a composed and detail-oriented person, found herself about to panic as she thought about all the things that needed to be done before her wedding. She missed her parents and knew if they were still alive they'd be helping her with all the details. *Thank God for Zoe.*

They'd been best friends since childhood, and she knew Zoe wouldn't let her down now. They were more like sisters than friends — they even looked alike, with the same beautiful blue eyes, rosebud lips and deep mahogany colored hair. It was sometimes difficult to tell them apart. She was glad they were living close to each other again. It had been hard to stay close when they'd lived in different states.

"Earth to Maggie. Have you been listening to me?"

"Yeah. I know, you're right. I haven't been focused. I'm working on it."

They drove through the village and found themselves passing the museum. Carol Pangborn had left Zoe a message regarding her research on the skeletal remains. Seeing the museum made her think of the sinister black ooze and ominous crucifix-covered box. *Just get through one more night,* she thought. *Father Mike will be here tomorrow to bless the house, and then everything will be okay.*

She knew everyone thought she was being silly about the house blessing. Garth and Maggie just couldn't get past their practical and pragmatic way of thinking. *I'm not crazy. There's something evil there. The Father will make it all go away and then I won't have to worry about it or being thought of as crazy anymore.*

A weary Father Fitzhugh sat in the Lord's sanctuary, keenly aware of what he would be up against the next day. He'd felt a supreme evil surrounding Zoe's home. It was only a matter of time before something truly bad happened there — the Dark One would not be held at bay for long. His minions were gathering.

The news he'd received from Rome was not good. The demise of several more catholic priests around the world had been reported recently. They'd lost their lives performing exorcisms and banishing demons, just like the one he'd face at Zoe's house. Father Fitzhugh had known some of the priests who'd been killed, and feared he might be next. *Beelzebub has been restless this year.* The old priest bowed his head and prayed he'd know what to do when his time to face evil as at hand.

Chapter 43

The great wolf had positioned himself on the small hillside behind the frozen creek, beyond the soft grass of the Avery's back yard. His great body blended into the winter landscape, making him almost invisible. His eyes were focused and alert.

Ancient instincts heralded the coming of the Fallen One. The wolf knew it wouldn't be long. He had left the man-dog earlier when the humans left. The wolf had watched as the man experienced the senseless killing and display of the deer. The evil one was playing games with the humans. His depravity came in many forms, all of which garnered disgust and loathing.

The sun shone high and bright this morning, and the wolf lowered his head in its warmth, resting for a while before the evil forces advanced.

Inside the house, Hugo lay nervously at the top of the cellar stairs. The black ooze had come alive again and kept trying to advance, only to retreat each time the dog growled. Evil now permeated the house, and the dog could feel it.

Hugo stayed steadfastly at the top of the stairs as the ooze taunted him, daring him to waver in his mission. With his hackles standing straight up, the big dog reasserted himself. He would not be intimidated and would not leave his sentry position at the top of the stairs.

Chapter 44

The Village was alive with shoppers filled with the spirit of Christmas. Tiny boutique shops, where traffic was sparse during the rest of the year, burgeoned with customers seeking out unique gifts. While there was cheer all around, the Christmas music playing through the town failed to lift Garth's uneasy spirits.

I haven't even thought about a gift for Zoe. It has to be special — it's our first Christmas together and our first in the new house. I just can't get past the feelings of doom. I'm starting to think Zoe is right about the evil. He was not a man to court foolishness. He was a pragmatist, a builder of brick and mortar edifices — solid and real, and it was difficult for him to admit true evil had taken up residence in his new home.

He walked into the local Ace Hardware and picked out a specialty mailbox. He opened the box to see that everything was in there, and then chose numbers and the rest of the supplies he needed for the project.

When he was done, he stopped for a quick lunch, again working to dismiss his foreboding. *Today I'm dealing with nuts and bolts — something real. That's all I'm going to think about*, he told himself resolutely.

Chapter 45

As they drove down the street, Zoe noticed that the bakery was open. "Right now! We're going to order your cake right now!" Zoe squealed.

Maggie abruptly stopped the car and both women dashed through the heavily garlanded door to take care of one more thing on the list for the upcoming nuptials. "It won't take long," Zoe declared, "we'll have plenty of time to see houses afterwards."

Maggie agreed. In truth she wasn't even sure if she liked any of the homes she'd picked out. None of them really thrilled her.

Their eyes grew wide as they took in all the goodies on display. The bakery was warm, inviting and filled with the aroma of pastries, hot cocoa and coffee. The girls ordered coffees and asked to speak to someone about wedding cakes.

They took their drinks to a table to wait. Both marveled at how it was starting to feel like old times between them. Zoe had even managed to dismiss the haunting sense of dread she'd carried with her since discovering that "thing" in her wine cellar. It was nice that they were able to have a lighthearted day doing things for the wedding.

Maggie finally made her cake choice after an hour of serious discussion about icings. Before they left, Zoe ordered croissants, bear claws and Napoleons to serve to Garth and Father Mike the next day. The girls left the bakery on a serious sugar high, laughing as they embarked on the quest for Maggie's "dream home."

It was nearly two o'clock by the time they pulled into the driveway of the first home Maggie wanted Zoe to see. By the time they reached the front door, Maggie couldn't even imagine why she'd wanted to see it. Everything was wrong. They both turned around and walked away without even going inside.

"Patience," Zoe coached. "You will find it when you least expect it. Look at how it happened to me."

"Oh, I know, Zoe, but look at all you've gone through. I don't know that I could take the punishment that old house has dealt you."

These were sobering thoughts for Zoe. No matter how much love she had for her home, she wasn't sure she'd be able to overcome the cancer growing inside its walls. These thoughts remained with her until they got back to her house.

When they pulled in the driveway, they saw the new wrought iron mailbox with "Mr. and Mrs. Avery" displayed boldly in gold lettering on its side.

This is my *home,* she thought with resolve. *I will not be bullied into leaving it!*

Chapter 46

Maggie dropped Zoe off, telling her to call after Father Mike's visit. "And don't forget you and Garth are coming over for dinner and tree trimming on Friday."

"We'll be there." Zoe waved as she watched Maggie head down the driveway, then hurried in to tell Garth how "wonderful" he was for putting in the new mailbox. "Love it, love it, love it!" she squealed to Garth. "It's beautiful. We are definitely official," she declared.

"Glad you like it. It was almost a crime to pay that much for a mailbox. Incidentally, I think I deserve a backrub tonight, setting your monument to mail has made me all stiff and sore."

"That can be arranged."

They ate a quick dinner made up of leftovers from Rachel's fantastic Thanksgiving dinner, and then watched the news as Zoe caught Garth up on

Maggie's real estate news and wedding cake choices. When the news was over, they snuggled close and watched an old movie.

Later, Garth lay in bed thinking about the coming day. He had a late morning meeting with Norm so they could go over several ideas regarding spring contracts. They wanted to walk the properties and get several issues nailed down before construction started in the spring.

Riza also always had some improvement or thoughts for updates on his Manhattan properties. Christmas and the holidays meant very little to a Saudi prince.

The bed felt better than usual tonight. Probably because it had been a long and pleasant weekend, filled with family. He missed Warren, Zoe's father. Losing him had left a void in Garth's life. Warren had been like a father, and he missed the occasional beer, golf, and fishing trips they'd shared.

Josh had begun to fill that void, though. Getting too close to anyone was unusual for Garth, but for Josh he'd make an exception.

He hugged Zoe close to him and fell into an uneasy sleep. Zoe slept no better. Other than a couple of nights of reprieve, restless sleep had become their norm. Both silently hoped this would come to an end soon. Zoe was sure it would end when the Father blessed the house.

Chapter 47

Garth got up early, and dressed appropriately for the construction site in his steel-toed boots, flannel shirt and jeans. Walking around the various projects would be good for him. Warren had taught him it was never too early to get a leg up on future contracts. That was one of the reasons his work was usually in on time and under budget.

Warren would be proud that they'd finally put the downtown project to bed, despite Beckman and his obstacles. Garth shuddered thinking of the past year. The prospect of starting the New Year fresh made him smile.

Zoe had started to stir, and Garth sat down beside her and told her he'd be home in the late afternoon. He didn't want to be late to meet Norm, so he got up and said, "I'll let Hugo out. Stay in bed for a while."

After he let Hugo out, he made coffee, poured it in his to-go cup and walked out the door into a cold, dry morning. The sun tried but failed to spread any warmth. Garth had used the remote start on the Jeep while his coffee was brewing, and its interior was toasty-warm.

As he got to the end of the driveway, he came to an abrupt stop. The new mailbox was laying on its side in a mass of twisted iron. *That prank had to take enormous strength and heavy-duty tools,* Garth thought as he got out to investigate. He said a few choice words as he viewed the destruction. Shaking his head in disgust, he decided to call Zoe and tell her about it later. *Is this the sort of thing you report to the sheriff?* he wondered.

After the deer incident, he thought it best to give the sheriff's office a call. He couldn't help but think about the laundry list of problems they'd had since moving to this house. He was finding it increasingly difficult to believe the bizarre incidents were random coincidence.

Passing the tiny chapel in the village, he thought, *Maybe it's good that Father Mike's visiting today.* Garth loved the giant leprechaun and his stories of the old country and Notre Dame football, but he still found it hard to believe that sprinkling a little holy water would make their troubles disappear.

He grimaced. He knew Zoe would shame him with a wag of her finger if she knew his thoughts on the subject. He was *not* a good Catholic. "Oh hell," he said out loud, "if holy water and a blessing is what it takes to fix things, I hope Father Mike has buckets full of both."

The longer he drove, the angrier he became about the mailbox. *It has to be someone targeting me, Zoe or the company. But why? If I didn't know that Beckman was dead and buried, I'd think he was up to his old sabotage tricks.*

Before he started seeing ghosts, he needed to talk to someone. He grabbed his cell and called Josh. "Can you meet me today?"

Josh noted the urgency in Garth's voice and agreed to meet him at one of their less frequented watering holes at four o'clock. There was no chit-chat or good-humored wordplay involved with this call, and that worried Josh. It wasn't like his friend to be so abrupt.

Chapter 48

The place Garth had chosen to meet Josh was packed for a Monday afternoon. The gray weather had apparently made people want to come inside for a drink. Reilly's was a man's bar and a bit old-fashioned. There was sports memorabilia hanging everywhere along with a rather large Canadian moose head that stared defiantly down on the blue-collar workers surrounding the bar.

A waitress named Peg, dressed in German attire sporting a low-cut bodice and extremely large breasts, was serving beer and wisecracks. Garth scanned the tables until he spotted Josh nestled in a corner booth, far too close for comfort to a dart-board and the drink-fueled contest that was going on there.

Garth motioned Josh over to a booth farther way from the game, and he picked up his Heineken and came right over. Peg noticed the move and nodded her head as Josh signaled and the pointed to his Heineken, requesting another.

She quickly returned with the order and commented to Garth, "You don't look so good. I'll bring you a Heine."

Josh noted the dark circles under his friend's eyes, too, and said, "Work isn't doing this to you, my friend. What's going on?"

"That's why I'm here. Since we moved into that damned house, I've lived with a sense of unease and worry. I can't sleep. Zoe can't sleep. I can't concentrate either, and I've been making mistakes at work. Norm and Mrs. Potter have been complaining that I'm preoccupied, and they're right. I'm not sure what's going on or what to do about it.

"Zoe has her boogeyman and demons theory, but she's been quiet about that lately, after I kind of made fun of her."

"You really should give her some slack, man. After your Revolutionary War friend was discovered, the idea doesn't seem quite so far-fetched."

"I know, I know, but the skeleton's gone, and I don't believe in leftover ghosts. But, things are getting worse, not better. Shouldn't they get better if it's his ghost and his bones aren't there anymore?"

Garth went on to tell the story of the gutted deer he'd found at the end of the driveway. "I was able to have them removed before Zoe saw. Then there's the mailbox destruction this morning. This was *not* the work of a kid on a bike. I don't know who could be doing this.

"Then there's the bugs, rats, snakes. The construction crew didn't like working on the house, either. They couldn't wait to get out of there. They could feel it, too. It's like it's alive, pushing back on every little accomplishment we have. This should *not* be happening, Josh. Everything should be good.

"There has to be somebody, a real person, targeting us. I don't know that I have any enemies left, now that Beckman's gone. Could you have Harry check into the mailbox and deer thing for me? Maybe the history of the house, too. I know Zoe's been talking to the lady that runs the little museum in town about that, but maybe he can find out more.

"I've been wracking my brain trying to think of somebody who might have an ax to grind with me. I can't think of anyone.

"Zoe's having Father Mike over today to perform his 'blessing of the house' routine. She thinks once he does that, everything will be great and we can put all this nonsense behind us. She's really looking forward to our first Christmas."

"Well, maybe it will work," Josh said, before his friend continued his diatribe.

"Call me quirky, but I think it's *someone* doing this, not *something*. They can't just disappear in a puff of smoke, so I think we'll eventually catch them."

"The thing is, Garth, I felt like that place was going to be trouble the minute you sent me down there to look at it with Zoe. I don't mean trouble as in possessed or haunted, but one giant white elephant that would cost you loads of money and aggravation. But she loved it. She didn't stop gushing about it the whole time we were there. You have to admit, she was right. You've got one beautiful piece of real estate now."

"Yeah, I guess so," Garth begrudgingly agreed and added jokingly, "if I could just quit hosting snake rodeos."

Josh chuckled as he started on his third Heineken.

An evil grin broke wide on Garth's face. "Hey, you're next with the house nightmares, pal! I heard the girls planning their next house-shopping expedition."

Josh's humor quickly faded as he lowered his glass in resignation, while Garth hummed the *Wedding March*.

As they got up to leave, Josh promised to call Harry and ask him to watch Garth's house for a couple of nights, plus do some snooping around to see what he could learn about the home's history.

Chapter 49

An older Mercedes station wagon drove up to the Avery home, and Father Fitzhugh emerged from the passenger side. The novice priest who'd acted as his driver got out as well. Zoe ran out to greet the Father and wrapped his giant frame in a bear hug.

Father Mike, ever protective of Zoe, couldn't help but show the concern he'd harbored about her house. The thought that she could be in danger was a heavy burden for him. He hoped this was just a case of stress and over-active imagination on her part, but knew it was probably wishful thinking since all of his research pointed to a marked rise in demonic activity. He reluctantly believed there was true evil residing in this home.

He took Zoe by the hand and introduced her to his associate, Father Tony Aveda. Zoe greeted him warmly, and invited them into the house. She quickly offered them hot tea, and a variety of éclairs and sweet rolls. The two priests sat down and gratefully took her up on the offer.

The Father hoped this visit would give him a better understanding of what he was dealing with. They had an interesting conversation regarding his new associate and how he came to be at St. Mary's, as they enjoyed the treats. After he finished, Father Mike picked up the basket he'd brought with him. In it was an object covered in a soft white towel.

"Consider this your housewarming gift," the Father said as he handed the basket to her.

Zoe took it and looked inside. There was a beautiful statue of St. Michael the Archangel, the warrior angel. The statue depicted a scene from the Book of Revelations and the angel, sword and shield in hand, was battling the dragon.

"Michael is God's highest in command, above all other angels in the army of the Lord," the Father told her. "He is champion of all Christians and the Church. Most of all, he will combat Satan and all demons serving him."

"Oh, Father, it's truly breathtaking." Zoe said as she lovingly unwrapped the statue.

Father Mike saw movement outside the French doors. He was a bit shocked when he saw dog and wolf standing side by side, asking to be let inside.

Zoe read the look on the Father's face and got up to let the unlikely duo inside. Hugo had only met Father Mike once before, but came up to both men, greeting each with a wag of his tail. The massive gray wolf came over next, and looked directly into Father Fitzhugh's eyes, seeming to touch his soul.

"You must be Invictus," Father Mike said, while he stroked the great beast's side. "I've heard all about you." A paw came to his knee, and Father Mike stroked it, too.

Zoe and Tony watched in awe and bewilderment. Neither could comprehend the bond between the priest and wolf. The only one who seemed to get it was Hugo, who had gone over to lie quietly near the fire.

Eventually, the wolf left the Father's side and went to sit quietly like he was waiting for instructions.

Father Mike stood and said, "Shall we begin our blessing?"

Zoe and the apprentice priest stood by, mesmerized. "What did you call him?" Zoe asked.

"Invictus. It means unconquerable. I've never seen him before, but I've heard of him. And, Zoe, I must say I feel like there's been a lot of good in this home. Perhaps a blessing is just what's needed to bring it back."

I hope I'm right about that, the Father thought before saying, "I think you should show me around."

"I'd love to, Father. Shall we start upstairs?"

Taking St. Michael with her, she led the two priests upstairs. Father Aveda was unusually quiet throughout the whole process. As she showed them the upstairs, she left her new gift at her bedside. "Perfect!" she said in a delighted voice.

Zoe then led them back downstairs, and took them through the den and Garth's office. After that, they went back through the great room and toward the open kitchen. As they reached the far kitchen wall and circular staircase, Father Mike stopped in his tracks. He was stiff, like a divining rod searching out water.

He saw the black ooze on the side of the circular stairwell wall. The stuff seemed to draw back from him as he got closer. "I don't think it's necessary to go below," he said. "We'll stay right here and pray."

All three made the sign of the cross, and bowed their heads. Father Fitzhugh began, "Lord, let there be health, purity and strength here. Goodness and mercy and the fulfillment of the law shall abide here. Thanksgiving to God, the Father, and to the Son and the Holy Spirit. May this blessing forever remain upon this home and all who dwell herein, through Christ our Lord, Amen."

Father Mike retrieved a small bottle of water from his pocket, uncapped it and liberally sprinkled its contents on the sullied wall and down the circular stairway, while cleansing all around in the Latin vernacular. "Now, young lady, I think you mentioned a box filled with the articles you discovered?"

"Yes, Father. It's still outside. It's been taped and re-taped, and covered with my crucifix, just like you told me."

"Good! Father Aveda and I will take it with us. It shouldn't be near your home."

"That's fine, Father. Please, take it. Mrs. Pangborn from the village museum did some research on the items. She found letters from that period, and townspeople spoke of a Cecil Bradford. He was a bloodthirsty and hated man. I think the items belong to him. They might be of historical value to this community, so I think the museum should have them."

"That's good to know, Zoe. We'll take them back to the sanctuary and see what happens from there. Now let's pray that things will look up for you from this day forward."

Father Mike being the good Catholic priest he was, turned to her and requested a glass of sherry.

Chapter 50

Tuesday morning, Josh woke Harry at about 10 a.m., just as he was thinking about embracing the morning light peeking through his blinds. He was not an early riser. He stretched his massive hand and grabbed the phone when it rang. An irritated growl emerged rather than hello.

Josh knew his friend wasn't a morning person, so he was brief. After listening, Harry said, "I'll see you about one o'clock."

Never one to move too quickly unless he had to, Harry rolled over and decided to get a few minutes more shuteye. That didn't last long, as curiosity about what Josh wanted and Nature's call drove him from his bed.

Reluctantly he opened the blinds to a new day. After a shower and shave he'd be ready to take it on. As the morning progressed, his level of curiosity heightened. Josh usually had some high-profile client or celebrity he needed background on, but this time he'd indicated it wouldn't be the usual job. That was all right with Harry. That Beckman fiasco had been enough intrigue to last a lifetime.

He went to the kitchen and made himself a cup of black coffee, then cleaned up after himself. For a bachelor, Harry was very neat and had great attention to detail. He didn't like a mess, so he also had a cleaning lady come in every week and today was her day.

He left her a note and also asked her to pick up his dry cleaning, which she would do happily. He was her favorite client because she didn't have to do much work at his house.

As he walked into Josh's office he, as always, was turned out in true sartorial splendor. Not a wrinkle, not a smudge, shoes shined, glorious gray hair perfectly groomed and cut. Today, his blue tie matched his dancing blue eyes. "What's up, kid?" he asked as he plopped himself down on the side of Josh's desk like he always did.

"You look like you're right out of a Bogart movie. You know that?"

A big leading-man grin spilled over Harry's face, and he chuckled. "What did ya need me to do for ya?

Reluctantly, and almost sheepishly, Josh said, "You remember when they found that bag of bones over at Garth and Zoe's house in the Hamptons?"

"Yeah. And?"

Josh explained everything, from the workmen's unease in the house to the illness, and the bugs, rats and snakes. "They can't sleep, and they've both have a general feeling of uneasiness. I had a beer with Garth yesterday. He said Zoe thinks the house has got some kind of evil entity or vengeful ghost attached to it. She's called a priest in to bless it and everything.

"That's not why I called you though. He told me about some things that don't sound ghostly at all." He filled Harry in on the deer and mailbox issues and then said, "Weird stuff has been happening, there's no doubt about that. Garth thinks there's someone behind what's going on. He can't believe it's because of anything paranormal."

"Let me see if I understand. You want me to investigate a broken mailbox, sleepless nights, and dead deer?"

"Well, not exactly. You've got to look at it from their point of view."

"Josh, I don't do ghosts!"

"I know how it sounds, but you know Garth. He's a pretty settled guy. It took a lot for him to even admit he thinks someone might be targeting them. Could you check on the history of the house and see if there's something that points to someone who might have it in for them because they bought it?

"Garth said Zoe was checking with the local museum to see what she could find out, but you're a lot better at that sort of thing than she is."

"My fee's the same whether it's a person or a ghost. I wouldn't do something this crazy for anyone but you, kid."

"Thank you, Harry. At least we'll all have something to talk about come trout season. Oh, did you get the wedding invitation?"

"Yes, and I look forward to it, even though it means another good man bites the dust."

"She's a gem, Harry."

"Yeah I know, Josh. They're all gems, until—"

"Until what, Harry?"

"Just until," Harry insisted. "I just love all women. The freedom and choice of it all is exciting. I'm not one to be tied down."

"Just wait, Harry. You won't leave this life unscathed."

"Well, maybe, but 'til then I'll enjoy the chase and escape! I'll checkout any hooligans hanging around Garth's place and let you know what I find."

Chapter 51

Garth's welcoming committee was overwhelming as he stepped through the door. Zoe greeted him with a giant hug. She was beaming. Garth hadn't seen her this animated for at least a month.

The house was warm and cheerful and that sense of gloom and doom that had been getting him down seemed to be gone. The smell of freshly cut pine permeated the air. Even Hugo seemed more relaxed, and his post at the top of the cellar stairs was left unguarded.

"Isn't it beautiful?" she cried as Garth's eyes strained to reach the top of the tree. "Have you ever seen a more perfect tree? After Father Mike left, I called Rach to see if the boys could come over to set it up.

"Lech just got his driver's license, so he was happy to drive over and help. I can't believe those are the same children we saw a year and half ago. The twins are almost as big as Lech. I hope Beckman is no more than a distant memory for them.

"I'll have to get some more decorations. I don't have nearly enough for this size tree. There aren't many ornaments left from when I was little."

Garth sat quietly, unable to get a word in edgewise. Finally, when Zoe took a breath, he jumped in before she could get going again. "Well, obviously you had a good day."

Without missing a beat she launched into the details of her visit with Father Mike, talking about his new associate and the beautiful statue of St. Michael the Father had given her. "He took that awful box of things from the cellar, too. I'm glad to be rid of them. I also scrubbed down that black stuff on the cellar wall after he left, and it stayed clean this time."

"The day went beautifully, Garth. Father Mike seems to think that his blessing and prayer will bring comfort and peace to our home. I'm so glad. I've been worried about my sanity lately. What with those awful nightmares, the infestations and feeling weak all the time — it was all getting to be too much. I just had an ominous feeling about this place

217

and I couldn't make it go away. Thank goodness for Father Mike!"

Zoe threw herself onto the sofa next to Garth. He pulled her closer, and hugged her tight. He decided to keep his ominous secrets to himself.

Hugo looked up approvingly at his two masters. Even his uneasiness had subsided in the wake of the Father's blessing, and goodwill seemed to fill the home.

"Where'd his wolf buddy go?" Garth asked.

"Oh, Garth, you wouldn't believe it. The wolf went right to Father Mike like he knew him."

She got up and went to the French doors to see if the wolf would come in. As the large, blue-eyed beast came over to greet Garth, Zoe said, "His name's Invictus. At least that's what Father Mike called him. I can't believe the way he was with Father Mike. It was like they were old friends. Father Mike said, 'You must be Invictus,' and the wolf responded."

Hearing his name again, Invictus made several circles, as canines do, and took his place next to Hugo. Garth was still mystified by the sense of peace the animal brought with him.

Zoe and Garth both sat quietly, content to enjoy the comfort of the fire and each other. Eventually the tantalizing smell wafting from the kitchen caught Garth's attention. "Trying another one of Rachel's recipes?" he queried, sniffing the air appreciatively.

"How'd you know? This is a new one. It's Beef Bourguignon — beef in red wine sauce. I got it from her this afternoon. She's better than the internet when it comes to recipes. Come on, I'll set the table. Dinner in ten?"

"Oh, yeah. I'm starving!"

For the first time in a long time, peace reigned supreme in the Avery household, and warmth surrounded them both. While Father Mike's blessing cleansed the home of lesser demons, the bigger evil still lurked below.

Meanwhile, Father Fitzhugh prayed his blessing and prayer were enough to keep Zoe and Garth safe. *Satan doesn't give up easily, and there was definitely evil in that house. Perhaps I got to it in time and this will be the end of it. I cant' be sure, though. The evil one might've pulled back to fool us. The denounced angel is a wily one. He's been known to retreat, stay*

silent and regain his strength before attacking again.
I wish I could be sure, but only time will tell.

Sleep came reluctantly to the old priest as he repeatedly prayed for Zoe and her household. He prayed that the devil might yet again be banished from a dominion he forever covets.

Chapter 52

Harry called on Tiffany for the task he'd been given by Josh. She was his sometime secretary and girl Friday. Chasing down vandals and punk kids wasn't exactly his thing. So, while Tiffany spent computer and library time checking on the home's history, he would check with the local authorities regarding teenage crime and mischief.

Harry found out there wasn't much heavy-duty crime in this part of Long Island. However, this area was not immune to the drug epidemic. The local authorities seemed to know who the "bad boys" in the area were, but there were no reports of vandalism, smashed mailboxes, or animal cruelty.

All in all, Harry found that the area around the Avery's home was pretty quiet. There'd been several speeding tickets, reports of rowdiness, and some DUIs earned by tourists checking out the foliage and visiting wineries, but nothing serious or mysterious.

Tiffany, on the other hand, found out the area was rich in Dutch/German folklore and Indian mysticism, plus much of the Revolutionary War was fought here. She also researched violent events that had happened within a five-mile radius of the home.

The computer in the small town's library belched copious amounts of info. It seemed this area of the Hudson River Valley, Peekskill and the Catskills Mountains was a kind of mystical nexus. Books were filled with stories of dreaming Rip van Winkles and marauding types akin to the Headless Horseman.

Accounts of strange happenings, two-headed toads, and witches brewing potions abounded. She found documents detailing both real and imagined events. She also read stories about the area's American Indians, both their kindness and their savagery toward the settlers and soldiers. This information filled pages in several books, and reading these kept her enthralled for hours.

Harry, on the other hand, was about to give up and christen this village the most perfect little hamlet in the world. Hardly anything bad seemed to happen here. Discouraged, he stopped by a local establishment to grab a cold one and rest his feet. When he came in, he noticed the young deputy he'd met earlier sitting at the end of the bar.

It was a slow Tuesday afternoon, and happy hour hadn't started yet, so patrons were sparse. Harry called Tiffany to let her know what he was doing and she told him she was still engrossed in reading about the history and lore of the area. "Give me an hour and I'll meet you there," she said distractedly.

This gave Harry time to talk to the deputy and maybe get a little "unofficial" information. "Bartender, give that man another of whatever's he's drinking — on me," he said, indicating the off-duty deputy.

"Thought you'd be headed back to the big city as fast as you could," the deputy commented.

"I'm just sittin' here soakin' up the local atmosphere, Deputy Harris." Unbeknownst to Harry, this was also the deputy who'd answered Garth's call about the dead deer.

"This is a good place to do it," he said, and moved to sit next to Harry.

Harry and Joe spent the next hour and a half talking. Harry learned a lot during this casual conversation.

Joe agreed with his conclusion about the area's crime rate. "There's no doubt we're virtually crime free, but if you're looking for unusual reports, we have crank calls at least once a week."

Joe made a quick reference to the call last week about a bunch of deer with their throats cut and left on a resident's driveway.

Harry quickly acknowledged that the man who'd called was a friend of his, and he'd told him strange things had been happening since he and his wife moved to the area.

"Oh, he's the guy that found the skeleton in the basement, isn't he?"

"That's the one."

"Caused quite a stir around here. See, that's what I mean, Harry — no crime, just strange stuff like that all the time."

Tiffany showed up just as he finished speaking, carrying her computer and a briefcase full of research. She sat down on Harry's other side, and announced she was ready for a drink.

Harry made a quick introduction to his new friend, and signaled the bartender for another frosty glass.

Tiffany took a long drink from the glass, set it down and announced she was starved to death. Both men looked at each other, recognizing this was pretty much an order to get the woman some food.

Joe took the lead and led them around the corner to his favorite little steakhouse. The laughter around the table was contagious — Deputy Joe was funny as hell.

He told them he'd lived in the area his whole life, except for the short stint he did in the Air Force. He said he'd tried for pilot, but his eyesight and depth perception kept him from getting in, so he did his stint and came home to the deputy job.

After he finished telling his life story, he launched into tales of the many unusual happenings around his community. He kept Harry and Tiffany entertained all evening.

Harry picked up the tab in payment for all the deputy's information. He liked the kid and was happy they'd met.

Harry and Tiffany soon left the quiet little hamlet for the bright lights of New York City.

Chapter 53

Harry wasn't a golfer, but he agreed to meet Josh and Garth at a club they frequented. Harry hadn't seen Garth for a year, and they greeted each other enthusiastically. Garth remembered the help Harry had been during the Beckman fiasco, and truly appreciated it.

"Good to see you again, Harry." Garth said, then got right to it. "I know Josh has told you about our 'situation' up here, with the strange things happening and all. I haven't gotten a good night's sleep since we moved in.

"Zoe thinks it all has something to do with bad karma or evil possession or something. I don't believe in that nonsense, but I have to keep the peace. She's even had a priest bless the house to banish all the evil she thinks is haunting us.

"I can't find any concrete evidence of anything else going on and I can't think of anyone who has a grudge against us, so she's almost got me believing her theories. What's stumping me is, who would do these sorts of things? I don't think we've made the neighbors mad."

"Harry, we were hoping you might find something in the history of the house, or a rash of incidents similar to this reported to the police," Josh interjected.

The waitress came to take their order, interrupting their discussion. They decided to go ahead and have lunch while they continued their talk.

After the waitress left, Harry began a little hesitantly, "You know, I got to know the local deputy pretty well at the tavern the other day, and he told me some interesting stories. He's a nice kid. He's also the one who answered your call about the deer."

"I remember him. He was nice enough to take care of it before Zoe saw the carnage."

"Well, we had a good long talk before Tiffany showed up. This is a nice, quiet community, Garth. There's not much crime, and there's very little drug activity. The only things going on are speeding tickets and maybe some occasional pot. More than likely it's the tourists that come through that cause the most problems.

"But," Harry went on speaking with a twinkle in his eye, "Deputy Joe tells me that a lot of people in the area call in with strange sightings. Quite a few of them involve apparitions."

Garth gave him an incredulous sideways glance.

"You heard me: app-a-ri-tions," he emphasized. "You know, ghosties, spirits and the like. Local police records going back 50 to 60 years list all kinds of complaints like that. Trouble is, you people are living in an Enchanted Forest Zone — Rip-Van-Winkle territory. Beware of toads, trolls and poisoned mushrooms.

"Tiffany found loads of Indian legends as well as Dutch/German folklore related to this, too. As a matter of fact, there were several sightings of ghosts, including an Indian roaming the hills, a soldier, and a blonde girl in a blue dress and white apron. All were written off as drunks or residents with overactive imaginations.

Josh, of course, had heard a lot of these tales during his childhood. Most of the local kids had heard about the headless horseman, and brought him up every Halloween. He wasn't surprised to hear about the numerous ghost sightings, either.

"All the ingredients for a great ghost story are here," Harry continued, "though the local authorities haven't heard much about the witch living at the edge of the woods lately.

"Garth, I wish I had something more concrete to report. This is New England, and the ghost stories are everywhere. Tiffany found reports of areas that should be avoided, and some of them are close to your house. There were also lists of bridges that shouldn't be crossed at night, saying 'danger lurks for any horseman that passes.' Most of them don't exist anymore."

Harry lowered his head and used his best gather 'round the campfire voice to whisper the next bit of information. "One of those bridges was located near your home. It was called the Mayfair Bridge, and it had a reputation for never letting a man return home if he crossed it at night.

"Tiffany found old maps showing the places townspeople said to avoid after midnight. Your house is in one of the 'hottest' spots for all this superstition and folklore stuff from 1700s clear into present times.

"There was also a place called Hangman's Hollow, where the British hung traitors to the crown.

The hanging tree was located near a mystical well that was mentioned several times. It was called the Well of Wickedness. The legend says that anyone who drank from it was destined to live a life of misery and despair. ... I could go on and on."

Josh and Garth both found themselves mesmerized by the stories, just like a couple of kids. "Jeez, Harry, I've lived here most of my life and I never knew about all of those stories," Josh responded with awe.

Harry snapped both of them out of their reverie by announcing he had to get back to the city. "I'm sorry I couldn't help, Garth. I don't think there's anyone around here who has it in for you, so you don't have to worry about that. Tiffany did love doing the research for this job, though. She said I should give her more assignments like that."

"Thanks for looking into it, Harry.

"Hey, Josh and Maggie are dropping by on Thursday to decorate the tree with us, why don't you and Tiffany come by, too? We'll let the girls decorate and us guys can sit around and drink beer. What do ya say?"

"Well, we'll see. Too much country air makes these city lungs itch.

"As to the other stuff, I wouldn't discount Zoe and her priest. It couldn't hurt, and things just might get better for you. If nothing else, it will keep the peace between you and Zoe."

"Well, maybe," Garth conceded.

Harry smiled and got up to leave. He was a good Catholic and knew a blessing from a priest could lend strength to one's courage.

Little did Harry know, what Father Mike was up against was something far more sinister than curses, legends and apparitions, and it didn't live in the enchanted forest.

Chapter 54

"Come on, Hansel, we better be off to see the wizard, too," Josh said, getting as much mileage as he could out of the last hour of conversation. "We don't want to end up at the Hangman's Tree. The girls will be looking for us."

Garth and Josh parted ways, as Garth thanked him again for helping to looking into everything for him.

Maybe it was just nerves, Garth thought. *The house, plus all the projects I've finished this year, plus Beckman and the murders last year, contractor setbacks, and the financial pressure. Maybe it's been harder on us than we realized.*

Garth was starting to think maybe he could relax a little. The house was finished, Zoe was healthy, their profit and loss sheet was looking good, and their future looked bright. *I'm a lucky man.*

As he drove through the village, he decided to stop at the local grocer and buy a bottle of Zoe's favorite wine and some flowers.

The late November sky was dimming, and a flurry of lacey snow softly whirled its way down the middle of the road as Garth drove home. For the first time since they'd moved here, he was really happy.

Chapter 55

The old English Tudor had a glow of warmth surrounding it as Garth drove up and eagerly walked to his front door. The night was cold and dry, and the smell of pine and burning hearths filled the air. Garth inhaled deeply as he checked the sky above him. It felt good to be alive.

He opened the door and greeted his wife with a whole new attitude. He was glad to be home. "Woman of the house, where are you?" he bellowed in a playful tone.

Zoe came running to greet him. "What is it, man of the house?" she asked, as she noticed the flowers and wine. "What did I do to deserve this?"

"Nothing yet, but I'm sure you'll think of something," he said with a wide grin.

"Oh, I'm sure I will," she said as she relieved him of the flowers and wine. "How about we crack this open, watch the news, and then you can tell me all about your day. It must've been a good one for you to bring me flowers."

As she popped the cork, she noticed Hugo coming through the door. His wolf companion was nowhere to be seen. The big dog trotted directly to Garth, greeted him and then lay down in front of the fire.

Zoe poured the wine and handed a glass to Garth. "I'm happy you're home early tonight," she announced, as she settled in by him. "How was your lunch with 'Mike Hammer' and Josh."

Garth had told her he was meeting Harry and Josh, just to catch up on man talk and planning their next fishing excursion. He also told her he was going to talk about the mailbox incident.

Zoe knew Garth was still brooding about its destruction. "Well if it was kids, I hope they find them and let their parents know. That was a beautiful mailbox. You couldn't have found a better one to match the house."

"Well, Josh had Harry snoop around the area to see if he could find anyone responsible. Harry being Harry, he was thorough. He checked to see if things like this had happen around here before. He also checked into all of the weirdness we've experienced since we moved here. He even had Tiffany check local legends and ghost stories at the library while he talked to the locals. Apparently, we live in an almost crime-free zone.

"He also met our local deputy and had a couple of beers and dinner with him. Harry said the deputy confirmed his crime-free findings."

"Well that's wonderful to hear."

"The bad news is we're living smack-dab in the middle of 1700s folklore at its best. According to Tiffany's research, we're surrounded by a magical forest full of ghosts and goblins. The Deputy said they get lots of reports of ghosts and strange sighting all the time, which seems to make the stories more legit."

"Well, you know, when I first saw this place I felt like it was straight out of a Disney movie. I opened those French doors, and it was a scene straight out of Bambi. It was beautiful. The deer, the babbling brook — it was magical! So maybe it's fitting that we live in a magic forest.

"I think the Father's blessing has fixed whatever was wrong in the house. I haven't felt this normal and happy in a long time." She reached up kissed him on the cheek and snuggled in close.

"By the way, I invited 'Mike Hammer' and Tiffany to help decorate the tree. They probably won't show, though."

"That's fine, the more the merrier. I haven't seen those two since Rachel's bash last year. Seems to be quite a May-December romance going on with him and Tiffany," she mused.

"Now, Zoe, don't you go trying any of that matchmaking stuff. Tiffany works for him, that's all."

"Oh, all right," she pouted. "Anyway, there's only one romance I'm interested in right now." She got up and gave him her best "come hither" look, then led him up the stairs with promises of good things to come.

Chapter 56

Morning found Garth and Zoe wrapped in each other's arms. Sleep had come gently and quietly, and they'd both slept through the night. The tormenting nightmares and restlessness had finally left them.

Garth was first to greet the daylight, and felt the urge for a morning run. He quietly grabbed sweats and a sweatshirt and slipped out, letting Zoe sleep. When he got downstairs, he became doorman of the day for Hugo, and then made coffee so it would be waiting for him when he returned.

He put on his clothes and shoes and headed outside. A wall of frosty air slammed him in the face and his breath made clouds as he warmed up for his run. As he started down the driveway, he hoped there were no unpleasant surprises waiting for him.

The coast was clear, and his body came alive as he started running. Heart pumping and blood surging, he ran a couple of miles, then headed back. As his feet fell, he thought about the fact that a year ago he was unable to move. He knew he was blessed and was feeling good to be alive.

Thirty minutes later, the end of his driveway was in sight, and his thoughts turned to replacing his mailbox, again. *Damned kids*, he thought. *They'd better leave it alone when I get it put back up.* He decided he'd put the project in motion later in the day.

By the time he reached the front door, his mind was busy making a list of the things he'd need for the mailbox project. When he came in, he saw that Zoe was up and cheerily pouring a cup of coffee for him in his favorite mug. She seemed full of Christmas cheer and smiles this morning.

"Been thinking of replacing the mailbox today," he said, accepting the mug from her.

"That sounds like a good idea," she replied absent-mindedly. She was already thinking about shopping with Maggie to replenish her Christmas coffers. "Hmm, let's see, wreaths, white twinkle lights, four garlands and some red ornaments. Christmas is not Christmas without red and green," she said, talking more to herself than Garth. "We'll also need wine and treats for tonight."

"I guess you're not too interested in my plans for the day," he joked.

"Oh, that's not true. Do I need to put anything on my list for you?"

"No, no, it's too late to heal my wounded feelings by offering to buy me things," he continued. "Everything I need is at the hardware store. I dare say you girls won't be going there today."

Zoe chuckled and said, "No, that's not a stop we've planned for today. Maggie will be here around 9:30, so we can get an early start. Oh gosh, it's already nine! I better get dressed." Zoe sprinted up the stairs, and left the man of the house chuckling and sitting down to finish his coffee.

Chapter 57

A shiny new mailbox sporting gold letters spelling out "Mr. & Mrs. Garth Avery" greeted Maggie and Zoe when they returned at four that afternoon. Zoe couldn't believe it — this mailbox was actually better than the first one. It had a black filigree post with wrought iron curlicues and a horse's head. It was a perfect style to complement their house.

Maggie helped Zoe unload her treasures and then quickly left, saying she'd be back at seven.

"Remind Rach she's welcome to come," Zoe said, as her friend got into her vehicle.

Just as Maggie was pulling away, Garth opened the door to see if he could help carry in the loot.

Zoe handed him several bags and boxes, then said, "Oh, Garth, the mailbox looks wonderful. It's prettier than the first one."

"I lucked out," he said as they both heaved bags inside the door."

"I knew you'd like it the minute I saw it. Finding it was the easy part. Getting it into the ground was way harder."

"I have no doubt, but all your hard work has paid off. Our grand dame looks wonderful. Just wait 'til you see it when she's dressed for Christmas!

"I bought a few bottles of wine for tonight. I know it's silly, but I haven't been downstairs since the whole skeleton mess began. Can you take them to the cellar for me? Even though the black stuff seems to finally be gone, it still kind of creeps me out down there.

"Maggie and Josh will be here about seven. We'll just nibble on cheese crackers, sliced salami and what not, then later we'll dig into the huge pot of chili I made last night."

"Oh, Harry called. They're coming. I didn't really think he would, but Tiff can't wait to see the house. Apparently she gave him no peace 'til he said he'd bring her here."

"That's great! We have plenty of food and I'd love to see them again. Plus, that means more help decorating the tree."

That evening, the fire glowed warmly and the house was filled with activity and laughter. It felt the way friends and family should feel around Christmas.

Zoe proudly showed the house to Tiffany, being sure to describe the awful condition it was in the first day she laid eyes on it. She also told her everything they'd done to get it to the condition it was in today. After she heard all the details, Tiffany had a few stories to tell about the area.

She related tales of horrible men with missing hands, tragic stories of missing children and Indian plagues, then graduated to more lighthearted fare that included fairies, leprechauns, and magical dwarves that made wishes come true.

"Well, this place has been anything but magical," Garth offered. "It was more like a nightmare!"

"Told ya, buddy," Josh countered, in his best attorney voice.

"Next time, counselor, I'll take your advice more seriously. Zoe and I were beginning to think this place was cursed after all the trouble we've had."

"Oh stop it, Garth," Zoe said in defense of her home. "Look at it, it's the Mona Lisa of houses now."

They all toasted in agreement, and Zoe added, "Call me superstitious, but I did have Father Fitzhugh — you know the one who's performing Josh and Maggie's wedding — bless the house. He was here the first of the week and he also gave me the beautiful statue of St. Michael that was on the nightstand in the master bedroom."

"Enough talk!" Maggie interrupted. "Let's decorate that tree and open up the season with a few Christmas carols and eggnog."

A little while after they'd started decorating, Hugo barked to be let in, and he brought his friend along. Harry and Tiffany looked on in amazement as both animals came quietly inside. Both extended their hands to pet the animals. "Is this what I think it is, Garth?" Harry asked, while stroking the beast's head.

"It is, Harry, it is. He showed up about a month ago and now he comes and goes as he pleases. He and Hugo seem to be friends."

The wolf and Hugo quietly slipped over to the corner of the large room and sat down close to the fire. Tiffany whispered, "I just said hello to a wolf. Maybe you guys *do* live in an enchanted forest."

Maggie just shook her head. "You'll get used to it. Maybe you just need another glass of wine to steady your nerves."

Armed with bows, tinsel, ornaments and garlands, the girls went back to work. They started off with the best of intentions at the base of the tree, and worked their way up. However, they were all relatively short, and in the end they had to ask the guys to finish because they couldn't reach the top of the tree, even with the ladder.

When they were finished, they all stood back and admired their handiwork. It truly was a magnificent tree.

By 11:30, everyone was ready to call it a night. After they left, Zoe sat down on the sofa to admire the tree while Garth started cleaning up.

Chapter 58

After tidying up, they headed upstairs at about 1 a.m. The day had been long, and sleep came quickly. The two didn't stir until late the following day.

Garth woke to a clawingly cold chill embracing his shoulders and chest. Groggily looking down, he found the heavy down comforter was still in place. This fact cleared his sleepy mind and he was instantly alert. He looked around and noticed that the windows were shrouded in a thin frost.

Deciding he needed to investigate further, he got up and threw on a heavy sweater and socks. He then nudged Zoe. "What is it?" she whispered, shivering.

"Looks like the heat's gone out. I'll go check the breakers and furnace."

Zoe quickly got up, put on some warm clothes and followed him downstairs. They were met by a halo of icy blue mist that made it difficult to see across the room. The light they'd left on before going to bed wasn't lit, so Garth made his way to the switch on the wall. He heard a whimper before he got there and asked, "Hugo, is that you?"

Straining to see, he followed the sound of labored breathing to his beloved dog. "My God, Zoe, get the car. *Now!*"

The dog's big brown eyes looked lovingly at Garth as he scooped him up from the pool of blood he was lying in.

Zoe opened the door and they ran to the car. Garth set Hugo on the back seat, and climbed in beside him.

"Closest vet! Closest vet!" he shouted to Zoe as she started the car. "Call the sheriff, too."

Zoe called 911 and was transferred to the sheriff's office. Deputy Joe answered, "Yes, Mrs. Avery, I know where you live. Bring him to the vet here in town. I'll call and let him know you're coming in with an emergency, and I'll meet you there."

Dr. Moore was waiting and prepared as Garth, eyes overflowing with tears, gently set Hugo down on the stainless steel table. The doctor's assistant immediately ushered him out to the waiting room.

Head in hands, Garth tried uselessly to understand who would do such a thing to an innocent animal.

Joe tried his best to console both of them, assuring them that Doc Moore was the best. "Your dog couldn't be in better hands."

Zoe called Maggie to let her know what was happening and then she called Father Mike. "Father, I know the Church's feelings about animals and souls, but please pray for our sweet Hugo. I believe God has a place for animals, too."

Joe stayed with them until the doctor had finished surgery. He came out to talk to them and announced that all that could be done had been done. "Your dog had lost a lot of blood. He's sedated now and I'd like to keep him overnight. We'll monitor him and by tomorrow we should know more. There's nothing more you can do here today, folks. Why don't you go ahead home and I'll be in touch.

"By the way, what exactly happened here? That's a killer wound. It almost looks like something tried to gore him. I've only seen wounds like that when treating stock animals."

"You need to tell me what happened," Joe said quietly.

"Could we do that at our house, Joe?" Garth asked.

"Sure, I'll follow you there. Mrs. Avery, are you able to drive? "

"Yes, I'm fine, deputy."

"I want them caught and prosecuted! They were in my home," Garth bellowed.

"I realize that, but I think we should wait to discuss this privately. I'm still not clear on what happened."

"I'll take a look around and see if there are any signs of a break in," the deputy said when they'd exited their vehicles in the Avery's driveway.

Just then, Maggie and Josh pulled up and got out to check on their friends. Garth and Josh went with the deputy to check outside the house and Maggie and Zoe opened the front door to go in. Two ravens flew out as the door opened, and the stench of rot wafted through the open door to greet them.

When they walked inside, it seemed dim in the house, even though the sun was shining outside. They gasped when they saw the tree — it had turned brown and was covered in rotting, foul-smelling ornaments.

Zoe saw that Invictus was standing at the top of the cellar stairs with his teeth bared. His hair was standing on end as he growled into to the emptiness below.

Suddenly, like the timbre of a bass drum, a voice came from the dark cellar. It was deep, hypnotizing, and sweet as molasses as it asked, "And how is that miserable, pathetic doggie of yours?"

Just as it spoke, the three men came inside, stopping short as they smelled the foul odor.

"You Bastard! How dare you hurt our dog!" Zoe screamed. "I know who you are," she said fearlessly as she ran to grab her bible. "Show yourself."

Waving the good book, she taunted and mocked the voice, ordering it to come into the light, as the others looked on in stunned silence.

Slowly and almost imperceptibly, a wisp of swirling smoke appeared. Seeing this, Zoe commanded, "Get out of my home! You and your kind are not welcome here. Go to hell and stay there, you sniveling, incompetent, inept, irrelevant fallen angel! You are of no consequence in God's world."

Each insult hurled at the mist made the figure solidify more and more. Like a poisonous, bloated toad, it kept growing larger.

"Fight me, you coward! Or, do you only pick on defenseless animals?"

The shape answered her with a sickeningly sweet voice, "But it felt so good, Zoe, seeing him writhing and whimpering in pain. All of that blood pouring from his body was just glorious. It was stupid of him to try to protect you from the likes of me. It was my pleasure to make him bleed."

Filled with a passion she'd never experienced, Zoe called the entity out again. "You are nothing more than a lowlife coward, preying on the weak and defenseless. You are the epitome of cowardice. You are a worm beneath the Lord's feet. Be warned — there are no cowards in this house. You will not win!" she shouted as she brandished the good book like a sword.

The evil had reached full power, and Zoe stood small before it. Garth grabbed her and pulled her away before it could harm her.

Suddenly, as if by divine direction, the light and force of St. Michael appeared. He stood in full battle raiment, with Invictus by his side.

Unbeknownst to those witnessing the battle, Father Fitzhugh had arrived. He hurried through the door and joined the others, staring in wide-eyed amazement. St. Michael, looking substantial and mighty compared to the mist-made specter, spread his wings wide. With sword drawn, he descended to meet the threat, and the battle began.

The sound and fury surrounding the fight between Good and Evil seemed to rage on for a lifetime, but in truth it was over in a heartbeat. Zoe was right — the devil was a coward and beat a hasty retreat when he came face to face with God's mighty soldier.

The Warrior Angel had reduced Satan's minions to a hissing pile of waste in the middle of Zoe's kitchen floor. When he was finished, St. Michael looked into the wine cellar and pointed his sword into the darkness. A great light exploded from the blade, racing to eradicate the evil below. The light exploded in a bright flash and then all was silent.

That done, the warrior touched his sword to the evil that remained in front of him and it exploded in a flash of blinding white light and was gone. Turning to the amazed humans, he smiled and then purified the whole house with a sweep of his mighty sword. Suddenly, the ruined Christmas tree burned bright and was made beautiful again.

The Avery home was once again filled with light, life and warmth, and St. Michael's job was done.

Silence and disbelief filled the room as six astonished people stared at the space where an archangel had just stood. When they had recovered slightly, they all noticed the wolf had remained to comfort them.

Chapter 59

The awe-filled silence was broken by Garth's cell phone ringing. It was Dr. Moore, calling to update them on Hugo's condition. Garth listened anxiously, then broke into a smile as he was told Hugo was improving. Garth thanked the veterinarian and hugged Zoe tightly as he told her the good news.

He turned to the still recovering deputy and shook his hand, thanking him for his help.

Suddenly he had an epiphany, *"That's* what happened to Hugo," he said, pointing to the now cleansed basement.

"Just how am I going to put that in my report?" the deputy asked. "If I report the truth, they'll want to hold me for a psych evaluation."

The two men laughed and the young deputy gave everyone, even Father Mike, his card and told them to call if they needed anything. The deputy left soon after, still marveling at what he'd just witnessed.

Garth reached over and hugged Zoe. "I'll never doubt you again. I promise."

"And you won't call me a religious nut, either?"

"Never," Garth said sheepishly as he looked over at the old priest. "Sorry, Father."

"Nothing to be sorry about, my son. I hardly believe it myself. I guess we won't need an exorcism. Zoe and her angel seem to have handled everything quite nicely."

Turning to Maggie and Josh, he said, "I'll see you two next week to finish up the wedding discussion. I've got to get back to the church now." He shook Garth's hand warmly, said good-bye, and winked at him impishly. "It is rare that a convert is made in such an extravagant manner, but we do know the Lord works in mysterious ways. He must've known you needed a big push to find your faith."

Garth grinned broadly and thanked Father Mike. After that, everyone said their goodbyes and Zoe walked the old priest to the door. As they neared it, the wolf came forward. "Well, Invictus," the Father said, patting him on the head, "I've heard many stories about you over the years. I'm so glad to have met you in person. You take care of these good people." Turning to Zoe, he said, "I'll see you next week."

Shortly after, Maggie and Josh left, leaving Zoe and Garth to contemplate the happenings of a day they would never forget.

Chapter 60

From that point forward, there was only joy in the Avery household. For the first time in months, Garth and Zoe felt like their lives were normal.

Zoe had asked Father Fitzhugh to send the box of Revolutionary War items they'd found to Mrs. Pangborn at the museum. She hoped the items would be a welcome addition to the town's collection, and was relieved that the last of the items connected to the evil Colonel were gone from her life.

The following week, Rachel, Zoe and Maggie hung around Rach's large kitchen island, laughing and planning the wedding. The Lawton household, too, felt reborn. Rachel and the boys had decorated their home and it was fairly exploding with Christmas splendor.

Everyone in Rachel's circle was celebrating life. She was happy that Josh had found Maggie, the boys were healthy and out of danger, and on the road to being fine young men, and Rachel had filled the hole in her heart left by her late husband.

With all the planning involved, outsiders might think the upcoming wedding would include several hundred guests. However, invitations were sent to only 40 close friends and family. Everyone was eager to witness the nuptials, since Josh had previously been a confirmed bachelor.

Josh suddenly realized the man he'd only known for a little over a year was now his best man and best friend. Having Garth and Zoe around to help deal with the wedding stress had been invaluable.

Father Fitzhugh had counseled Maggie and Josh for their future and life together, and was confident in their choice to marry. "Life has many roads and detours," he told the happy couple, "but you can face anything life throws at you by working together and keeping God by your side. Do that, and all will be right with your world."

Hugo was slowly recovering under Dr. Moore's care. Zoe and Garth came to visit him often while he was staying at the animal hospital. A few days later, when he was stable, he was allowed to return home. There was a laundry list of things needed for his care, but neither Garth nor Zoe minded.

When they got him home, Garth brought him inside and put him on a new cushioned dog bed next to the fireplace. Invictus was at the door immediately, and Zoe let him in so he could lay down beside his canine friend. The two maintained their strange bond, even though the evil had been banished. Zoe wondered if Invictus was waiting until Hugo was healed before moving on.

In the weeks that followed, Hugo mended nicely and was walking with barely a limp.

Late December cold had settled in to upstate New York as Deputy Joe made his rounds. He saw Garth shoveling his driveway and pulled over.

When Garth saw him, he asked, "Why don't you come in for a cup of coffee? Zoe's been baking, and there's a lemon pound cake."

It was an invitation the deputy couldn't refuse. Once inside, the two men stuffed themselves with cake and chatted amiably.

Suddenly Invictus stood, ears alert. The great gray wolf nuzzled in close to Hugo and dropped his head. Then he walked quickly over to Garth, with Hugo following. The great wolf extended his paw in a rare moment of affection, first to Garth and then to Zoe, his eyes meeting hers.

That finished, he moved to the French doors he'd passed through so many times during the last two months and asked to be let out. Zoe, as always, obliged.

Once outside, the great beast turned back and looked at them for a moment, then bounded toward the soft sound of wind chimes. Zoe wondered if this was the call telling him he was needed elsewhere.

Hugo stood by the doors with Zoe and watched Invictus meet a translucent figure. "Garth, Joe, quick, come look at this."

The three stood spellbound, watching the strange tableau. The figure had solidified into a young woman with golden hair. She wore a blue dress and white apron, and her hair was tied with blue ribbons that matched the cornflowers she carried.

The girl knelt and spread her arms wide, inviting Invictus to step into the hug. Smiling, she held onto him for a moment before rising. Invictius then led her through the forest and into the sheltering pines.

Joe ran after them, only to find undisturbed snow where they'd been. "Well, I guess this proves it. You really do live in an enchanted forest," he said with wonder.

"If that's the case," Garth replied, "then we intend to live happily ever after."

The End